Praise for
free verse

★ "Dooley subtly exposes readers to poetic forms
that invite engagement, understanding, and expression,
while Sasha and her extended family are depicted
with a sweetness reminiscent of Cynthia Rylant—
a southern soulfulness that is warm even as it reveals
the downtrodden struggles of a mining community."

—*Booklist*, starred review

★ "The changes in [Sasha's] life, the anguish
she feels, and her journey forward are expertly
portrayed through Dooley's use of first-person
narration, which is sensitive and gentle without
being soft or sentimental. The poetry is wonderful
and feels authentic to Sasha's years."

—*School Library Journal*, starred review

★ "In this gripping story, Dooley balances a clear-eyed
depiction of families wrestling with addiction, financial
stress, and trauma with the astonishing resilience of
children and the human capacity for love."

—*Publishers Weekly*, starred review

"Sarah Dooley mixes poetry and prose to powerful, poignant effect in her novel *Free Verse* . . . This story brims with hard-won insight into the travails and small joys of life."

—*The Washington Post*

"Sasha is a natural with words. They bubble out of her, spilling emotions onto paper that she couldn't otherwise articulate. And as she experiments with different forms, Sasha discovers poetry's double blessing: The structure stabilizes her, while the creativity sets her free."

—*The Christian Science Monitor*

"The story mounts a quiet defense of the nobility of broken people . . . who hold on when all seems lost and sacrifice much out of love for their children."

—*The Bulletin of the Center for Children's Books*

"Dooley winningly combines engaging plot twists and rich character development with the introspective and thematic power of poetry: not to be missed."

—*Kirkus Reviews*

"Dooley shows readers the richness of small-town life . . . Tween fans of realistic fiction will find depth in this novel."

—*VOYA*

"This novel is a triumph of art over loss, a story that will make you believe in the capacities of poetry."

—Gary D. Schmidt, author of
Newbery Honor–winning *The Wednesday Wars*

"*Free Verse* is . . . a startling book, surprising at every turn, and its exploration of poverty, trauma, and loss deserves to be read by as wide an audience as possible."

—Daniel Handler, Lyn Miller-Lachmann,
Neal Shusterman, and Susanna Reich,
judges for the 2012 PEN/Phyllis Naylor fellowship

ashes to asheville

ashes to asheville

sarah dooley

G. P. Putnam's Sons

G. P. Putnam's Sons
an imprint of Penguin Random House LLC
375 Hudson Street
New York, NY 10014

G. P. Putnam's Sons is a registered trademark of Penguin Random House LLC.

Library of Congress Cataloging-in-Publication Data is available upon request.
Printed in the United States of America.
ISBN 9780399165047

1 3 5 7 9 10 8 6 4 2

Design by Michelle Gengaro-Kokmen.
Text set in 11.25-point Berling LT Std Roman.
This is a work of fiction. Names, characters, places, and incidents either are the product
of the author's imagination or are used fictitiously, and any resemblance to actual per-
sons, living or dead, businesses, companies, events, or locales is entirely coincidental.

For Heather and Jennifer,
whose heads are flat rocks.
I would NOT be writing this dedication
even if you weren't here!

chapter

1

Right before my sister, Zany, steals our dead mother off the mantel, I'm trying to decide which sock to stuff in Haberdashery's mouth to shut him up. He's barking every five seconds, *yip yip yip*, all shrill like a smoke detector with its batteries low. It's a wonder Mrs. Madison hasn't come downstairs in her slippery cheetah robe, waving Mr. Madison's ancient handgun. She keeps the thing in her purse, says a widow as pretty as her needs protection, especially with, what she calls it, her *assets*. I thought she was talking dirty the first time I heard that, till Mama Shannon explained she meant money.

Before Zany reaches for the mantel, my biggest problem is whether to sacrifice my left sock, which is blue and belongs to Mama Shannon, or my right sock, which is purple and was Mama Lacy's. I miss both my mamas. I don't want to give up either of their socks, but how else am I going to shut this dog up before Mrs. Madison wakes to find that my sister's broken in?

I've pretty much decided on Mama Shannon's sock, both because Mama Shannon is alive to wear other socks and because I'm a little bit mad at her, even though I don't want to be. When Zany reaches for the mantel, I'm still holding the blue sock in my left hand, all foot-shaped and the bottom covered with Haberdashery hair. But I'm not still thinking about the yipping dog, although he's in a tizzy now that the midnight intruder has proven to be a thief.

"We're not supposed to touch that!" My whisper falls in between Haberdashery's yips, and it's loud as sandpaper on splintery wood.

Zany eases Mama Lacy's curvy brass container down off the mantel and clutches it to her chest. I don't like the word *urn*. I can see it rising and falling with her uneven breath. Even in the half dark, I can make out the smile across her lips. Grinning and breathing hard and doing something crazy, that's why Zany gets called Zany instead of Zoey Grace and that's why she's not supposed to drink more than half a Mountain Dew per day. But this might be the craziest thing she's ever done.

"Mama Shannon says only followers do what they're 'supposed to,'" she whispers, "and Culvert women are born leaders. Come on." She starts for the door, and I follow her, even though I know Mrs. Madison is going to freak out if she wakes up and Mama Lacy and I are both gone. I follow her, even though Haberdashery panics when he sees the door swing open, and starts tugging on my remaining sock. I wonder whether Madison women are born followers, because the truth is, all I ever do is follow Zany. She always knows the way.

The night air is a shock to my system. That's what Mama Lacy would have called it: "a shock to the system." Mama Shannon would say it was "colder than a witch's toe." Or a witch's something else if she thought we kids weren't close enough to hear. Mama Lacy and Mama Shannon couldn't have been more different in how they talked. They were so different, I thought it was a wonder they ever managed to fall in love.

After living with Mrs. Madison for months, it's easy for me to understand why Mama Lacy always talked so fancy. There are entire sentences Mrs. Madison says that I don't understand. Stuff like, "Kindly escort me to the sitting room," or, "Be a dear and please grant me the pleasure of your company at the breakfast table." Stuff

3

that would make more sense if she didn't clutter it up with all that fancy talk.

The brass jar is glinting in the weak light, and I follow it through the darkness. It's cold enough to steal your breath. It's still February for one more day, and Zany didn't exactly give me time to change when she committed *Grand Theft Mother*. I'm dressed in a slippery bubblegum-pink robe Mrs. Madison bought me over my flannel PJ pants and a yellow Milk Duds T-shirt that belongs to Mama Shannon. I'm still only wearing one sad purple sock.

Zany isn't dressed much warmer, but hers is on purpose. Low-cut tank top, tight-fitting jeans, clunky boots, and a sweater that looks like it's made to show off the tank top, not to actually keep a body warm. Still, when Zany sees me shiver, she pulls off the sweater and swings it around me, and it's cozy from her arms. I hold it close and I feel the oddest thing, since Zany is right here in front of me. I feel homesick for her, the same way I feel for Mama Shannon, who I hardly ever get to see, and for Mama Lacy, who I won't ever see again. My feet stumble to catch up to my sister. I don't hold her hand, because I'm twelve, but I wish I could.

At the end of the drive is Mama Shannon's car, and that's when I know this isn't going to be any quick thing. I don't know how I thought Zany got here. I guess I didn't think about it. I'm not so good with the details. Mama Lacy was always smoothing my hair and telling me, "You can focus better, Fella. I know you can." Mama Shannon's wording was a little less delicate: "If you tripped over a dead body on the floor, you'd say 'pardon me' and keep right on walking." Which might be true—there was that time I said "Excuse me" to the parking meter when I bumped into it with my elbow and I thought it was a person—but I don't like having it pointed out. It's not that I don't try to pay attention. It's just that there are so many things to pay attention *to*.

"Where we going?" I ask.

"Remember the ice creams, Fella?" Zany changes the subject as she unlocks the car doors. I think it was pretty responsible of her to remember to lock them. I have no idea what she's babbling about, all I know is that the seats are freezing when I try to sit, and I don't want to think about ice cream right now.

"What ice creams?"

"The ice cream bars at Mack and Morello's."

I lower my butt to the seat, then hitch it back into the air. Still too cold.

"I remember Mack and Morello's, but I don't think I remember ice cream bars."

Zany pauses with her hand at the ignition and gazes

past me for a minute. I wish she'd turn the key so the heat would come on. I'm getting tired of hovering above the seat. "They had two flavors, Heath bar and strawberry shortcake. I liked strawberry shortcake because it was pink, and you liked Heath bar because it wasn't." She turns the key at last. I like how Mama Shannon's car engine sounds. It's rough and warm. It's got a different voice than other cars. I hear it and I hear Mama Shannon's own voice, talking up in front while I'm dozing in the back. I miss her so much.

"No, I don't remember that." I don't mean to sound annoyed, but I do anyway. Zany is sixteen, so she's got four years more memories than me. But even the memories we share, she remembers better. I remember what the purple door sounded like at Mack and Morello's, the way the bell jingled extra loud if I came in at a run. I remember an orange floor and something about dropping a hot dog.

"Why are you thinking about Mack and Morello's?" I ask.

"You know your seat's never going to get warm if you don't put your butt on it."

"Yuh-huh, the heat will warm it up."

"Yeah, maybe by the time we get there. Nothing in this car works all the way like it's supposed to." Zany puts the car in reverse and starts down the driveway. She twists to look over her shoulder and I twist to look at her.

"Get where?" I latch on to the important part of her words.

But she ignores the question. "Put on your seat belt."

I turn to reach for my seat belt, and I catch a glimpse of something moving in the darkness outside the car. Something fast and familiar and extremely pesky.

"Wait!" I roll down my window and hear yipping.

Zany hits the brakes. "How'd that dumb thing get out?"

"He must have run out when we left. He's always doing that. Zany, I have to take him back!"

Zany studies the upstairs windows, still and dark. "You can't do that. He's too loud. And anyways it's always when thieves go back that they get caught." I'm surprised she owns up to being a thief. Then I realize she's including me.

"We can't steal him, too," I protest.

"It's not stealing. We'll be back before anyone's awake."

My hopes fall. I guess I sort of thought Zany was here to steal me.

The view from the front is different from where I

usually ride in the back. I slowly lower my rear end to the cold seat, and I open the door and let Haberdashery in. He yips approval and climbs into the back, where he immediately gets to work making the seat comfortable by pawing at the fabric.

Zany backs down the driveway again, and I feel a little panicky at the thought of doing something as big as running away, and then coming back at dawn and getting caught. What if Mrs. Madison catches me sneaking Mama Lacy's ashes onto the mantel? Zany is cradling the brass jar in the crook of one elbow while she steers with her free arm. I ought to reach over and take Mama Lacy before she gets dropped, but I can't make my arms move. I've never held my mother's remains before and I don't plan to start now.

Zany puts the car in drive and we start down the darkened street. Even though I'm certain we're either going to go to jail or get in trouble with Mrs. Madison—and I am not sure which is worse—I feel a thick excitement at passing the MADISON DRIVE sign. Mrs. Madison isn't the only person who lives on Madison Drive, but hers was the first house here and remains the biggest. As far as I understand it, the city had to name the street after my great-grandfather to convince him to sell his lawn for development. I haven't been off this block in months, unless it was in a school bus or on our tense visits to church. Even though there's a shiny gold car in her garage, Mrs. Madison doesn't drive. Twice a year, a man comes to take the car to the mechanic for a checkup. I don't see the point, since that man is the only person who ever gets behind the wheel, but Mrs. Madison says a lady must take responsibility for her vehicle. She sounds about a thousand years old when she says it, and Mama Shannon always rolls her eyes if she's there. If she's not, that's when Mrs. Madison starts muttering about "that woman" Mama Lacy took up with, who lets her tires run down to the cable before she ever buys new ones.

"That woman" is Mrs. Madison's name for Mama Shannon. And it's true. Mama Shannon does let the tires run down to the cable. She also forgets to do things like get oil changes until the sticker on the windshield says she's late by at least a whole month. And her glove box is full of tickets—for parking, for speeding, for forgetting to put the right stickers on the outside of the car. She and I are a lot alike in that way. It used to drive Mama Lacy crazy how forgetful me and Mama Shannon could be.

Still, I don't see that it's Mrs. Madison's business how Mama Shannon treats her car. So I'm happy to get off Madison Drive, but my stomach is in knots because I also don't want to get in trouble. I still haven't gotten in real, huge trouble at the Madison house and I don't know what will happen. Will I get lectured? Ignored? Sent to bed without supper? Mrs. Madison seems formal enough that she could probably write me a ticket or send me to detention or something. Or maybe she hides what Mama Lacy called "a volatile heart" beneath that slippery cheetah robe and she'll get mad and yell and scream at me. My stomach feels wilty at the thought.

"Zany, I don't think we should be doing this." My excitement tips back over into panic.

Zany rolls her eyes. "You always say that about everything. And you're too late. We're already doing it." She spins the wheel at the corner and juggles her armload of urn, at last pushing it toward me. I try not to take it, but Zany lets go. If I don't catch it, it'll fall. It sinks into my palms, heavier than I thought it would be. It's almost as heavy as one of the weights Mama Shannon uses when she's stair-stepping.

Zany hits the gas once we get out on the main road. She turns on the radio, cranks the volume, and sings along to a tune that sounds as pink as my robe, all about falling in love. Gross. I clutch my dead mother to my chest, all cold and brass, as we escape through the night.

chapter
2

There's a picture on the dashboard of a perfect family: two parents and two kids, all girls. It was taken in 1999, the year we moved back to West Virginia from Asheville. You can't tell by looking, because our eyes are full of smiles, but already it was the beginning of the end of good things for us. Five years have passed since then, and not a single one has been easy.

We loved Asheville. I might be the youngest person in the family and have the poorest memory, but our love for our home, I'll never forget that. It wasn't just something we felt. It was something we talked about. Mama Shannon was always going on about how back home in West Virginia, she couldn't do this and back home she couldn't do that. But in North Carolina, in Asheville, she could do and be and say whatever she wanted, and nobody would get upset with her for it. She wore cargo shorts from the men's section and got her hair cut at the barbershop and she talked openly with anyone who asked about her love for Mama Lacy and the city they'd chosen.

Mama Lacy's love wasn't as loud. But she used to watch Mama Shannon with a smile on her lips. She used to nod at the right places in Mama Shannon's stories— "Back home, we couldn't find a church that accepted us as a lesbian couple." *Nod.* "Back home, we didn't want to send the kids to school knowing they were going to get teased for having two mothers." *Nod.*

Zany used to nod, too, seriously, as though she understood. Maybe she did. Zany was old enough to remember moving *to* Asheville, not just *from*. We moved to the city in 1994 when she was a first grader after Mama Lacy and Mama Shannon realized our neighbors in West Virginia weren't ever going to like us.

In Asheville, our family was accepted. Though it wasn't legal there or anywhere else for my parents to be married, there were more gay people in the area and it was more accepted for them to raise kids and have families together. We were able to go to school there without much fuss—I remember a couple of dumb kids picking on me about my moms, but those were the same kids who picked on me about my tangled hair or my oversize rain boots that I'd stolen from Zany. And there were some substitute teachers who had a little trouble understanding. Overall, though, Asheville was kind to us.

Still, in between figuring out what they wanted to be when they grew up—something neither of my moms ever settled on—and going about their daily lives of squabbling and laughing and mopping floors and fixing dinner, my parents watched the news with hope.

"It's coming," Mama Shannon used to say when something good would happen in the news. When civil unions became legal in Vermont, when a politician would mention gay marriage during a debate, when other countries legalized it, Mama Shannon would get so excited she couldn't hold still. She would work harder on whatever project held her fancy at the moment—building footstools out of driftwood, sanding old chairs to make them look new again. "Picture it, Lacy! *Real* marriage is coming!"

I didn't like when she brought up those things, because it meant pointing out that the marriage they already had wasn't a real marriage. It sure *looked* real, just like the marriages on TV. They hugged and they fought and they danced and they kissed and sometimes Mama Shannon slept on the couch and sometimes Mama Lacy washed the same dish six or seven times while thundering under her breath, "Shannon's too daggone old to play guitar in a band" or, "Can't Shannon even see when there's no toilet paper on the roll? It wouldn't kill her to change it."

Sometimes they even fought about their wedding.

"I'm not getting married in a church, Lace."

"That's where weddings happen."

"Weddings happen all kinds of places."

"Well, *my* wedding will be happening in a church, so if you'd like to be one of the brides, you can waltz your happy butt into the church and act civilized for five minutes."

Mama Shannon grimaced. "Bride? I'm a bride?"

"What would you rather be? You're not a groom, are you? I never meant to get one of those." Mama Lacy bit the tip of her tongue the way she did when she was teasing. "I can think of some other names to call you. Which do you prefer?"

"I don't know." Mama Shannon was laughing now, too. "I'm your partner. I'm your . . . your significant other."

" 'You may now kiss the significant other'? That lacks the ring of romance, babe."

"Fine. Wife. We're wives. 'Bride' just sounds so . . . young." Mama Shannon leaned in toward Mama Lacy.

"I mean, *you* can be a bride. You're still young and beautiful. You can pass this old ogre off as your spouse, but you can't convince me I'm a 'bride.'"

They had dozens of conversations like this, and at the end, Mama Lacy would lean in to kiss Mama Shannon's hand or cheek or lips, and then Zany and I squealed that they were gross and would they please knock it off because there were children in the room. And they would break apart and pillow-fight us or tickle us until we thought we were going to pee, but Mama Shannon would always come back to the way things were finally starting to change.

"It's really going to happen," she would say. "We're going to be spouses, brides, whatever, in this lifetime."

Except you never really know how long a lifetime's going to be.

When Mama Lacy got sick with pancreatic cancer, we stayed in Asheville for a while. But soon, she wasn't able to work. It was cheaper to live in West Virginia, and Mama Lacy and Mama Shannon both had family here who could help with things like cleaning the house and watching us kids. The family wasn't perfect. Mostly, Mrs. Madison took me while Mama Shannon's mama,

Granny Culvert, who lived close by back then, watched Zany and helped with the house.

I remember being happy with Mrs. Madison in those days. Being in a family with a big sister with such a giant personality, it was fun to have all the attention on me for a while. Mrs. Madison taught me how to play games I was too young for, like bridge and poker. She taught me how to make snow angels, and peanut butter sandwiches with Marshmallow Fluff. At the end of each day, she used to wrap me up in one of her robes and plunk me on the sofa with iced tea if it was warm out, hot cocoa if it wasn't, and we would watch her game shows together. We were so cozy, I called her Grandma once or twice, though it never quite felt as natural as calling her Mrs. Madison the way everybody else did. She always glowed with pride when I could answer the questions on the TV before the contestants. Any time we met any of her friends out at the store, she would brag to them about the most recent thing I'd known that she didn't think a kid my age would. She was usually wrong—all the kids at school could do the same things I could do, and sometimes, more—but I never corrected her. I liked her to think I was special.

In the picture on the dashboard, I'm seven years old, and Zany is eleven and trying to lift me. My hair is in my face, but Zany's is sticking straight up. It's exactly like Mama Shannon's, short and white-blond. That's because Mama Shannon is Zany's birth mom and that's why Zany was able to inherit what Mama Lacy calls "the Culvert gene," which means Zany is as crazy as Mama Shannon and her family.

Mama Lacy is my birth mom, and she and I are Madisons. We're both quiet like cats and just as smart, at least that's what Mama Shannon says. It's hard to feel smart when you're always forgetting things, but Mama Shannon says that's how you can tell a smart person. They're too busy thinking about Big Ideas to worry about little details like tying their shoes or remembering their homework.

Mama Lacy says that Mama Shannon only says that because she's as forgetful as I am. Not Mama Lacy, though. She was really good with the details. She was good at remembering to take the car to the garage at the right time. She was good at signing permission slips and laying out matching school clothes and using up the vegetables before they rotted in the crisper. She was good at asking each person how their day was in a way that was unique to them so everybody knew she'd been paying attention the last time they talked. I will never feel smart the way Mama Lacy was smart, in a way that made her seem good at everything. She was prettier than anybody else, too. I got her stick-straight, dark brown hair, but she was always better at wearing hers, in loops and twists and braids that never seemed to come down no matter what she did in a day. If I braided my own hair, it wouldn't stay up more than an hour.

Of course Mama Lacy's hair fell out eventually, because of the medicine for her cancer. But even then, she wore scarves that matched her shoes and looked nice with the color of her eyes.

In the picture, Mama Lacy has her arms ready to catch me, if Zany should drop me. That's what Mama Lacy did, all the time, every day—she tried to catch me. Now that she's not here anymore, I feel like I'm falling and falling and I'm never going to land.

Zany's driving too fast for the one-lane road we're on and the photo is bouncing and flapping with each bump. I hold Mama Lacy tighter against my chest. I can't imagine anything worse than spilling my mother's ashes because of a pothole.

It isn't till we get past a sign that says we're entering a new county that I reach out and turn off the radio. The little dashboard clock says it's ten to ten, but I don't feel the least bit sleepy. Mrs. Madison goes to bed so early that, most nights, I lie awake for ages before I follow her

18

to sleep. Though Mama Lacy tried her best, we were never very good at bedtime in the Madison-Culvert household.

"My feet are cold."

Zany glances down and rolls her eyes. "Why didn't you put on shoes, Light Bulb?" She calls me Light Bulb because she says it's so rare that I have a practical idea, I ought to have a lightbulb that springs on over my head when I finally do think of something, like in a cartoon.

"I didn't know we was running away. Where we going, Zany?"

"You didn't know we *were* running away because we're *not* running away. We're taking a little trip, is all."

"You gonna tell me where?" The seat is finally starting to feel warm under me and Zany's cranked the heat up full blast in the direction of my feet. She'll tease me to death over something like not wearing shoes, but she always tries to fix it, too.

Zany reaches over and tugs my hair and then touches the shiny brass urn. "We're taking Mama Lacy where she wanted to go."

I think about this, but I'm not sure what it means. Did Mama Lacy have a secret vacation she wanted to take, one she told Zany about, but not me? I feel a pang of jealousy. Then of shame. Maybe she did tell me and

I forgot, like I forgot about the ice creams at Mack and Morello's. Maybe Zany is the good daughter and remembers things for Mama Lacy that I've forgotten.

We're at least a mile on down the road and I'm still thinking about what Zany said, worrying the inside of my cheek with my tongue and going through all the places I ever heard Mama Lacy mention she might want to go, when it hits me, like that stupid cartoon lightbulb springing on above my head.

"You mean where she wanted to be—to be—" I can't say *scattered*. Moms should never be scattered. They should, at the very least, be kept in one place. And they should preferably stay Mom-shaped.

Zany eases off the gas a little and fiddles with the cigarette lighter. "Of course that's what I mean."

After Mama Lacy died six months ago—*right* after, before all the craziness with Mrs. Madison—Mama Shannon read us the letter Mama Lacy had left for the three of us. It had our names on it, not our nicknames but our proper names, in her curvy writing: *To my beloved Shannon Culvert, and my sweet girls, Zoey Grace and Ophelia.*

Mama Shannon and Zany have been upset for a while because the letter went missing. They figure one of the cousins or aunts or even Mrs. Madison accidentally took it right along with Mama Lacy's pretty wineglasses and her father's wedding ring she wore around her neck on a chain. I feel heavy with shame at the mention of Mama Lacy's letter, which has been safe in my treasure box since the day Mrs. Madison came to take me. It isn't that I wanted to keep it from Mama Shannon or Zany. It's just that they had each other, and I didn't have either one of them, or Mama Lacy either. I wanted something she'd touched.

Over and over at bedtime, I take a minute to read the part she wrote for me: *To my Fella—my little sweets, you've got my hair and my smile and now you've got my family to care for. Be a brave girl and do a good job. I'm counting on you. Love you always—Mama Lacy*

She didn't know her own mother was going to come and take me away from Zany and Mama Shannon. She didn't know I wouldn't be with them to care for them. Though I begged Mrs. Madison not to take me, not to talk the judge into making me live with what he called "blood relations" instead of my own family, I feel like I've failed Mama Lacy somehow. I was supposed to take care of our family for her and instead I only see them on Sundays. I wish I could write her a letter and explain, or, better yet, curl up on her lap and play with her hair while I tell her all about it. But there's no way to talk to Mama Lacy anymore.

Anyway, Zany means the other part of the letter, the

part at the end where Mama Lacy explained what she wanted for her body. I only read that part once, but I can't make my brain forget it, even though the thought of cremation fills me with horror. Mama Lacy, who loved springtime and sunshine and high winds and thunderstorms, didn't want to be buried, to be closed away in a box, unable to breathe the air or see the sky. Of course she couldn't do any of that anyway, but Mama Lacy said the thought of being shut up in a box made her feel so sad and so still that she couldn't bear it. No, she wanted her ashes scattered across the grassy park next to our first home in Asheville, where she could smell the rain and see the sky and move along the earth like leaves with each gust of wind. She wanted to land where our feet landed when we played freeze tag and caught lightning bugs, when we turned cartwheels, when we ran with joy. I can't think about her words without my eyes flooding with tears, and for a moment I feel as though the whole world is nothing but waves of sadness.

The home Mama Lacy talked about seems so long ago and so far away, like it's not a real place anymore. I can't imagine ever running with joy, ever turning a cartwheel again. I feel like I'm heavy and all put together wrong. Nothing works right since Mama Lacy's been gone.

Mrs. Madison has never cared much for the out-doors. She went along with the part of the letter where Mama Lacy said she didn't want to be buried, but that was the only part she listened to.

"I won't lose her twice," she insisted. Her whole face was drawn up tight, lips pressed together till they went pale. "She'll stay right here in my home. I won't lose her twice." She moved a small glass bell with ALMOST HEAVEN, WEST VIRGINIA etched on it in gold, and three framed pho-tos of distant cousins I'd never met, and a beady-eyed deer carved out of coal, and she placed Mama Lacy right in the center of the mantel. With that taken care of, she set about the business of stealing me from my other mother.

Zany lights a cigarette and Haberdashery and I both start coughing. Mama Shannon used to smoke, but she quit when Mama Lacy got sick. Mama Lacy said the only good thing that came out of the cancer was it made Mama Shannon quit smoking. Mama Shannon started crying at dinner one time, which was shocking and scary because I'd never seen her do it. Mama Lacy led her quickly from the table, but I snuck behind and followed them down the hall to the door of their bed-room. Mama Shannon was upset that Mama Lacy had to be the one with cancer when she'd spent her whole life taking care of herself, eating healthy, running every morning, refusing to smoke. And Mama Shannon, she ate red meat and smoked a pack a day and drank beer a lot and talked about exercise she never got around to, and Mama Shannon was the one who was healthy as a horse. She cried and cried that night, and I sat and sat in the hallway, feeling cold and small.

"You shouldn't be smoking," I warn Zany. "It can kill you. Your lungs get all black and tough like leather and they shrivel up and they have spots on them. It's disgusting. I had a test on it in Health."

"We all took that test in fifth grade," Zany says. "You can't live your whole life afraid of pictures they showed you in elementary school. I mean, hell, it doesn't matter what you do. It doesn't *matter* what you do." So I know she's also thinking about Mama Lacy's healthy lifestyle, and she sounds so sad that I don't say anything else, not even to tease her when she chokes a little, then tosses the cigarette out, half-smoked.

I put down my window to air out the car. Haberdashery immediately jumps up behind my seat, resting his scratchy little poodle paws on my shoulder so he can stick his wet nose out into the fresh air. I reach back and lower his window down instead. I like animals fine, but Haberdashery isn't really an animal, more like another decoration in Mrs. Madison's big house. He doesn't get dirty or lick people's faces or chew up shoes or play with toys. All he ever does is sleep, and eat, and *yip yip yip*.

Zany makes a turn onto a different road, and then another.

"When did you decide to do this?" I demand. I hope Zany's thought this through. Ten or eleven more questions suddenly crowd into my brain and I start spitting them out in random order. "Do you have gas money? Did you bring road snacks? Do you even know how to get there? You suck with directions. I know you don't remember the way. Did you bring a map? Can you even read a map? Did you take the car to the garage and have them tell you if it was roadworthy?" I'm not sure exactly what roadworthy means, but I know Mama Lacy always insisted on getting the car checked for it before we left on a trip.

"Hush," is all Zany says. A minute later, she taps the glove box and it falls open. I catch the map that flutters out, then stuff all the bright green parking tickets back in. The map is printed off the Internet and in the dim light, I can only see a mass of tangled lines and numbers. I've never been good at reading these things.

Below is a list of directions to follow. They seem simple enough, and it says it should only take a little over four hours. I do the math, slowly, in my head. If we left

Mrs. Madison's just before ten, we should be getting to Asheville around two a.m. It shouldn't take more than a couple of minutes to scatter the ashes, and then we could be back in the car and on our way home. We could make it back by six a.m. For the first time, I feel a tiny pang of relief. Mrs. Madison doesn't wake up till seven at the earliest, and Mama Shannon's work schedule makes her a late sleeper according to Zany. We might be able to pull this off. Maybe Zany isn't completely crazy after all.

There's really only one problem with the plan, then.

"If we scatter Mama Lacy in Asheville, we'll never see her again," I say in a small voice.

Zany accelerates up the on-ramp, and for a minute she's preoccupied with merging among the coal trucks. Once we're on I-77, rolling along at seventy-six miles per hour, which is six more miles per hour than the big white sign says we're supposed to go, Zany reaches over and pats me, almost like Mama Lacy would. Her hands seem more grown-up than when I last noticed them. The nails are filed and painted, and there's no tremble, even with this big thing that we're doing.

"It's what she wanted," Zany says, so soft I don't have an answer, even if I'm not convinced.

chapter
3

After about twenty minutes, we take an off-ramp. It's way too soon to stop and pee, even for me, so I sit up and look around. When I recognize the road we're on, I start to bounce in my seat.

"Is Mama Shannon coming with us?" I ask. I can hear the hope turning up the end of my question.

I want Mama Shannon to come with us, not just because that will make the whole thing safer, having a grown-up along, but because I barely ever see Mama Shannon anymore. Just on Sundays for church and even then, she's not herself. None of us have been ourselves in the six months since Mama Lacy.

"No," Zany says sharply. "She's not coming, and we're going to be really careful not to wake her. In fact, you're not coming in at all. You're going to wait in the car. I forgot something. I won't be two seconds."

Hot anger whooshes up through my belly and out my mouth. "You can't tell me what to do!" But Zany ignores me and turns off the headlights, coasting through the darkness into the driveway. "Didn't you say it's when thieves go back that they get caught?" I remind her.

"Stay here," she says firmly, and she sneaks from the car.

I count to ten, then ten again, so she's got time to be out of sight before I follow.

Mama Shannon and Zany live on the bottom floor of a house. The top floor is a separate apartment, but there's still a door that connects the two. Mama Shannon has to keep it bolted or the upstairs neighbors will steal things. The first week, before she realized the door could be unlocked from the upstairs, Mama Shannon lost twenty-seven dollars and a maxed-out credit card from her wallet. She couldn't prove who took them, but she put a bolt on her side of the connecting door and it never happened again.

I've been inside the apartment before, but it still feels strange to me, in a way that my own mother's home shouldn't feel strange. I never lived here with Mama Shannon and Zany. They moved in after Mrs. Madison took me away. I can't help but notice, every time I'm in

28

the place, how different it is both from where I live now and from where we all lived as a family before.

When we were together, we lived in a few different places, but they all felt the same because they had the same stuff, and the same people. Mama Lacy always hung pretty things in the windows. Glass bottles, strings of beads, Christmas lights no matter the season. Mama Shannon's sweater was always slung over something or other.

This apartment doesn't look anything like one of *our* apartments. Nobody's taken the care to fix it up. The wood-paneled walls are dark and bare, not decorated with twinkling lights to make them brighter. The couch is a heavy brown color and isn't tucked under a familiar blanket. Instead, it's empty except for Mama Shannon, who sleeps draped over it with her feet sticking off the end.

Seeing her makes everything in me hurt.

She looks tired, even though she's sleeping. Her face has more lines than I remember, and her hair is tangled. She's snoring softly and drooling a little and I remember how I used to tease her for things like that, but I could never tease her when she looks this bad. I want to hug her, but she would wake up. I'm also mad, somewhere in my stomach, and I can't figure out exactly why. Something about not living with her anymore. Something about being left behind.

It takes me a minute to catch my breath, staring at Mama Shannon. I look at that brown couch and think about where I sleep, back at Mrs. Madison's. My bed is full-size and painted white. My sheets are flannel and the warmest thing there is. Mama Shannon isn't even using a blanket. I have to work to keep my eyes dry, because she always wakes up when I cry.

Zany sleeps in the only bedroom in the apartment. I make my way slowly, because the floor creaks something awful, and get to the door of Zany's bedroom as she's about to come out of it. She gasps but manages to hold in her scream, hand clasped to her heart. An instant later, her face goes from scared to angry and I know I'm in for it.

Still, even as she's gearing up to murder me, I can't help but look past her at her room. I know I'm staring. Every time I come here, I take in more of the details. The room is small and the walls are dingy white. Her bed isn't painted, because there isn't any frame. It's just a twin-size mattress and box spring sitting on the floor. Her window's got garbage bags taped over it to keep winter out. I see pictures taped to the windowsill: Mama Shannon. Mama Lacy. Zany. Me. We all look so much happier.

Something about seeing my own face on my sister's

windowsill makes my throat clog back up and the tears get harder to fight. I slip my hand into Zany's and she tugs me through the house. The carpet feels damp and gritty on my one bare foot. I see the small kitchenette with a mini-fridge and a bunch of cabinets with no doors. We pass the bathroom, which has only got a toilet and a shower stall, no room for a tub, and not even a mirror. The whole apartment would just about fit into my bedroom at Mrs. Madison's.

At the sofa, I pull my hand from Zany's for a minute. I know from the way she's tugging me that she's still upset about me being in the house, and I'm going to get an earful once we're out. But I can't help but stop and look at Mama Shannon, and Zany stops to look with me.

Mama Shannon is not what you'd call a peaceful person. It's so strange to watch her sleep. It used to be hard to catch her sleeping. She used to stay up till the rest of us were in bed, and it was impossible to beat her out of bed in the morning. Now every time I see her, she's either sleeping or looking like she needs to. I notice she's still dressed, wearing the shirt they make her wear for her second job at the grocery store. Mama Shannon used to build furniture for a living. Not just plain old furniture, but big wooden tables and chairs and bed frames with pretty carvings on the edges. It took her years to get up the nerve to quit her job at the phone company and make furniture full-time. Then, almost as soon as she did, Mama Lacy got sick and Mama Shannon stopped in the middle of an end table. She went to work at a cell phone store once we got back to West Virginia, and then took the grocery store job on top of that to make ends meet.

Mama Lacy had a few jobs over the years to make money, but the job she loved, which she did on evenings and weekends, was taking photographs on people's happy days—weddings and graduations and birthday parties. Even when she wasn't working, she was taking pictures of her favorite things. There are dozens of beautiful black-and-white photos in a box somewhere in the closet, of us growing up, of Mama Shannon laughing and trying to cover the lens with her palm. Mama Lacy was almost never in our photos. She was always behind the camera. At our old place, the last place where we all lived together, the photos covered the walls. But when we moved, they went into a box, and nobody's had the heart to bring them out again.

For a few seconds, I think about abandoning Zany's midnight mission and crawling onto the couch with Mama Shannon. The feeling is almost impossible to ignore. She would tuck her arms around me and hug me in that rough, tight way that only she can, and I wouldn't feel so much like I'd lost both my mamas anymore. Zany seems to understand, and, mad as she is, her arm goes around me anyway. She squeezes me close and I fit under her arm just perfect. I suck in one sharp breath and push my chin up higher. We leave together, just the two of us.

Outside, in the car, I can't stop thinking about the empty parts of the apartment we've just left.

"Where's all the furniture?" I ask. The place is even emptier now than I remember it being last time.

"Shh." She's reversing down the drive, headlights still off. She's breathing hard enough for me to hear.

"Where's the stuff Mama Shannon made instead of the ugly stuff that came with the apartment?"

"Shh."

I bite my lip and wait for her to feel like talking to me, but out on the main road, headlights finally springing to life, all she says is, "You were supposed to wait in the car."

I sniffle a breath in, huff it out in frustration. "It's my house, too." I'm not sure that's true. After all, I have flannel sheets and hot cocoa waiting for me across town, and Zany and Mama Shannon don't. But it has to be my house, too. It belongs to my mama and my sister.

I'm relieved when Zany doesn't correct me. Instead, she says, "Yeah, well, you could have gotten us caught." There's no anger behind her words, and after a minute, her voice comes again, softer. "I know it's your house, too. I know it is."

"Then tell me where our furniture is."

"It's gone."

"Where?"

I hear her breath wobble out, then suck in. "We sold it."

"All of it?" I hear my voice get shrill.

"We had to, Fella. Bills have to be paid."

"You could have sold something else. Or asked Mrs. Madison. She has buckets of money."

Zany snorts. "Mrs. Madison wasn't about to loan us anything. Don't you remember how hateful she was being when we moved here? And we don't take money from thieves anyhow."

I do remember, once Zany mentions it. I remember Mrs. Madison going on about how "that woman" Mama Lacy took up with wasn't going to raise her only grand-daughter in that filthy place. I remember how much I hated her back then. But I still hate her, don't I? She *is* a thief, one who stole me away from my family, and at least once a day, I think about how much I hate her.

Sometimes I even say it out loud. Once in a while, she hears me.

But now that Zany's talking about her in that angry voice, I'm thinking of Mrs. Madison buying me new clothes even though I only want to wear my old ones, and how we've had baked chicken and French fries nearly every night because it's the only thing I'll eat. I don't know what to say and it makes me mad.

"That's stupid," I blurt.

"Fella . . ." I can hear the irritation in her voice.

"You shouldn't sell furniture just because you don't have much money. I liked that furniture. I wanted it in my house when I'm a grown-up."

"Oh, and I suppose Mama Shannon should work three jobs to keep you from losing your future furniture. She already works twelve hours a day, Fella. She's already too tired to stand up straight." She hits the gas and the car hops forward.

I have to either cry or change the subject, so I ask, "What'd you forget?"

"Hmm?"

"That we went back for. What'd you forget?"

She reaches into her shoulder bag and pulls out Mama Lacy's camera by its strap. It's her in-between camera, not the super-expensive one she used for photo shoots for work, but not one of the cheap waterproof ones she took with us to the park or the county fair. This one is the one she used the most, her everyday camera. It dangles in Zany's grip, twisting with the bumps in the road, until she reaches over to settle it on my knees.

"She'd want some pictures of Asheville," she says. "She always took pictures on road trips. I can't believe I forgot her camera."

"Where are the rest of your pictures?" I ask Zany. "You used to have pictures up all over your room." Zany wants to be a photographer like Mama Lacy.

"I don't take pictures anymore. After *this*, I won't take any more."

My voice sounds small even to me when I finally get it to come out. "Why?"

She keeps her eyes on the road, both hands wrapped tight around the wheel. It takes her a long time to answer, and she's so quiet I almost can't hear her when she does. "Because there's nothing I want to remember."

chapter
4

The first mountain tunnel we drive through is lit with orange lights split by chunks of shadow. I'm torn between thinking the tunnel is pretty and worrying about the millions of pounds of earth and stone currently located above our heads.

At the deepest part of the tunnel, under the tallest part of the mountain, the radio, which we've turned back on for noise, loses its signal and fuzzes out. For a minute there's nothing but silence and static and the *whir* of tires on pavement and the distant blast of somebody's horn. I imagine I can hear breathing inside the brass container on my lap. It takes all my willpower not to throw the urn back at Zany, driving or not. But the breathing turns out to be Haberdashery snuggled tight against the back of my seat, down on the floor. He doesn't like the tunnel, doesn't seem to appreciate being buried under tons of mountain either. Right when he's about to panic, we burst out into clearer night and smoother highway on the other side.

We cross the state line at seventy-two miles per hour. In the darkness, white letters stand out bright against a blue sign: WELCOME TO VIRGINIA. I peer around, but it doesn't look any different over here. It feels like forever since I've been outside of West Virginia.

"I hope you know what you're doing," I murmur at Zany for maybe the hundredth time. I take Mama Lacy's camera from Zany's purse to distract myself. She taught us both how to use it, especially Zany because she was really interested, but me too because I didn't want to be left out. I snap a few pictures of the darkened landscape. The only brightness comes from several orange lights framing the road leading away from the tunnel, and I'm pretty sure it's not enough light for good pictures.

"Those are going to come out stupid," Zany says. "You can't take pictures in the dark without the flash."

I raise the flash and snap a few pictures of the glare on the inside of the windshield.

"Quit it!" Zany shrieks. "That makes it really hard to see, Fella! You're going to wreck us!"

"You told me to use the flash!"

"Well, now I'm telling you to quit it!"

In a huff, I put down the camera. "Are you sure we should be crossing state lines? Doesn't that make you like a federal kidnapper or something?"

Zany glances at me like maybe she hasn't thought of it this way before.

"I don't think it does," she says, but she doesn't sound sure.

"So I guess I'm an accomplice," I add. "And a dog thief. You've turned me into a dog thief!" With every new realization, my voice gets a little more shrill. "I'm only twelve and I'm going to go to prison till I'm thirty for dog-thieving! Not to mention riding in a stolen getaway car!"

"Cut the theatrics," Zany instructs, sounding exactly like Mama Shannon.

"When you lose the attitude," I shoot back, sounding just like Mama Lacy.

I would say more, but that's when Zany glances in the rearview mirror and then sits up straighter. I twist in my seat to look out the back glass and see what she saw, which is a police car behind us. My mouth goes dry.

"Are we getting pulled over?" I ask, equal parts hope and fear. I'm not sure whether it would be good to get pulled over and sent home, or whether we've already done enough bad things that we'd be sent to jail instead. I decide it's probably best not to take any chances, and I turn around and sit up perfectly straight like Zany, keeping my eyes on the road like she's doing, hoping the officer behind the wheel won't notice us.

"Why isn't he passing us?" Zany asks after a minute. She talks out of the corner of her mouth.

"Maybe because you're speeding," I suggest, also out of the corner of my mouth, so the officer won't see us arguing and decide to pull us over to break up the fight. I keep my fingers tightly wrapped around the urn, my chin up and my eyes on the road. But without moving my lips, I keep talking. "He's a police officer. He's not going to break the speed limit. You're going way above sixty-five."

Zany takes her foot off the gas so quick I think the cop car is going to rear-end us for a second. She presses the gas again, not so hard this time, and gets us rolling at sixty-five.

"How long has he been back there?" she asks again out of the corner of her mouth.

"I don't know, Zany, why are you asking me? I saw him when you did!"

"I wasn't asking you, I was just asking to be asking."

"Oh, well, did anybody answer?"

"You know, you're not helping anything by being snotty." She sounds awfully hateful for somebody who's trying to talk without moving her face.

"So-RRY!" I say in a tone that clearly shows how un-sorry I am. I'm proud of myself for not moving my lips at all while spitting out this bit of sarcasm.

"Would you shut up until the cop's gone?" Zany asks.

"Why do I have to shut up? Why don't you shut up?"

"If you shut up, I'll shut up! I can't shut up while you're still yapping at me!"

Haberdashery yips and pops up like a jack-in-the-box and we both scream, forgetting to speak through the corners of our mouths. I'm still twisted in my seat, trying to shove Haberdashery into the space under the backseat, where he can't cause any more trouble, when the police car puts on its lights and my heart starts hammering. I hear Zany gasp. She takes her foot off the gas, breathes deep, and reaches for the turn signal. I'm regretting my sarcasm now, and I send up a silent prayer that if the police car will pass us by, I will never be sarcastic again.

After a pause long enough that I have to stop holding my breath, the police car whips around us and takes off through the night in the other lane.

"Oh my god," Zany says. "Oh my god, oh my god, oh my god."

"Gonna be a great trip," I say, and slump lower in my seat.

chapter
5

We're doing okay until the coal trucks
start cropping up. They come in fives and tens and they
career around us like we're in a toy car instead of a
big, sturdy Subaru. Every time one of them passes us, I
clutch Mama Lacy so hard the lid of the urn presses into
my chest, leaving a mark. Once they're past, I hear Zany
sigh in relief, but it's never long before another batch of
trucks catches up. Everything's happening so fast and
I'm so scared I can't stop talking.

"Be careful, Zany, here comes another truck—"

And, "Watch out! You need to speed up a little, I think
that guy's going to plow us over, he's not slowing down!"

And, "Slow down! What are you doing? Oh my gosh,
oh my gosh!"

Until Zany finally gives me a *shut up* look and flips on the radio.

We're in between groups of trucks when I realize I've got another problem.

"Zany?"

She can't hear me over the radio, which has begun blaring traffic reports from somewhere ahead of us on the highway. I hear the time: just past eleven. It doesn't seem possible we've been in the car for barely more than an hour. I feel like I've never been anywhere except riding passenger to Zany's Big Idea. I reach out and flip off the radio.

"Hey! That might have been important!" She starts to turn it back on, but I block her hand. We scuffle over the controls and I catch the change tub just as we start to knock it over. It used to be a butter tub, but it's been balanced in the console of the car so long, most of the letters have worn off. We keep spare change in it for things like toll booths and parking meters.

"Zany, I have to pee."

"God, you're so crude! Can't you say you have to go to the restroom? Or you have to make a stop? Do you have to come right out with it like that?"

"It's true, though."

"And why didn't you go before you left the house?"

She's still trying to get her hand around mine to turn on the radio. By the time she does, the traffic report is over and somebody's talking about the weather. "Dang it, Fella! You made me miss it!"

"I didn't go before we left the house because I didn't know we were leaving the house until you'd already stole Mama Lacy! You never tell me anything. You expect me to follow you and find out as we go!"

"Nobody said you had to follow me! I wasn't planning on you tagging along!"

I feel a stab in my chest when she says this. I thought she came to get me, too, but I guess she only came for Mama Lacy.

"She's my mama, too, I should get to be there when she—" I stop. I still can't say out loud what's going to happen to Mama Lacy once we get to Asheville. She's been gone for six months, but she's also been on the mantel where I could see her every day. The thought of the last little piece of her being gone forever is bad enough without imagining not being there to say good-bye. I can't even imagine what I'd say. We didn't talk, me and Mama Lacy, not like me and Shannon talked. I miss her hands and her hair and her voice, but I can't think what I would say to her if I had the chance. My fingers clutch the urn so tight it starts slipping around in my sweaty grip.

We pass through another tunnel and I'm distracted for a moment by the flash of the orange lights above us and the way the radio fuzzes out. But when we emerge on the other side, we pass an exit and I shriek. "Zany! Why didn't you stop?"

"You'll have to hold it," she says. "We can't stop every ten minutes or we'll never make it back!"

"I can't hold it four hours!" I protest.

"I don't mean four hours, I mean one or two more exits. We have to put some distance between us and home first, otherwise you're going to want to turn around."

"No I won't!" Even though all I want at this moment is to turn around. I would even accept my cold, lonely bed at Mrs. Madison's without complaint tonight, that's how scared I am to be out on the interstate with Zany as the driver.

It's warm in the car and I take off Zany's sweater. When she's not looking, I toss it into the back for Haberdashery to snooze on. He immediately starts the work of making it comfortable, scratching at it with his sharp little poodle claws. In minutes, he's fast asleep.

The bathroom thing is becoming a problem. I'm starting to do what Mama Shannon calls my potty dance, wiggling and tugging at my seat belt.

"I had hot chocolate before bed," I say. "Right before you came and got me." I scan the road signs, hoping for an exit and fuming about Zany not stopping at the last one.

"I ought to just pee, right here. That's what I ought to do, since you couldn't be bothered to stop."

Zany shrugs. "Go ahead and pee. You're the one that has to sit in it."

I wrinkle my forehead and hope the poodle pees on her sweater, but I don't say anything else.

"Look, see?" Zany says after a while. "That sign says there's a rest area in three miles. We can stop there for a bathroom."

Then we whip around a long curve and see an ocean of taillights in front of us. There are a few other cars like us, but most of the traffic is big eighteen-wheel trucks. Zany slams on the brakes so hard we squeak, and the car behind us swerves to keep from hitting us. Traffic on the interstate is completely stopped. Occasionally the vehicle in front of us inches up a foot or two, and we follow, but I look at the same REST AREA, 3 MILES sign for almost ten minutes without us ever getting past it.

"Where are all these people coming from?" I ask. "It's the middle of the night."

Zany glances sideways at me. "It's barely a quarter past eleven. Not everybody goes to bed at dusk like you do."

"This is why you should have stopped at the last exit!" I finally explode, slapping Zany's arm. "I really have to pee!"

She yanks her arm out of reach and rubs it. "Don't hit me, brat! This is why you shouldn't have turned off the radio. I would have known there was traffic up ahead."

I squirm and wiggle and I finally take off my seat belt.

"Put that on!" Zany demands.

"But it's squeezing me!"

"Put it on, Fella! Somebody's already wrecked up ahead, and here you want to ride without your seat belt!"

"But it's going to make me pee on myself!"

"Ophelia Madison-Culvert, put that seat belt on right now!" Zany tries out her Angry Grown-Up voice and actually does a pretty convincing job of it. Sulking, I tug the belt into place and slide down low in my seat, arms crossed. Except it's hard to keep them crossed because of my slippery robe, and the fact that any pressure on my stomach makes me feel like I'm going to have an accident. I balance the urn and the camera carefully on my knees, well away from the danger zone.

A minute later the car starts to smell, and Zany whips her head around to stare at me. We've barely passed the REST AREA, 3 MILES sign.

"Oh my god, you didn't!"

I'm startled. I would have been asleep already if it wasn't for my bathroom situation.

"I didn't what?" I ask, groggy.

"You peed!"

I sit up straighter. "I did not!"

"Then what's that smell?"

We stare at each other for a moment and then turn to look at Haberdashery. He's asleep again, comfortable. But he's moved off Zany's sweater.

"Oh my god!" she shrieks. "Is that my sweater? Why did you give it to him?" She reaches back to grab the sweater and screams when her hand touches it. "It's wet! He peed on it! He peed on my sweater! Why didn't you give me back my sweater if you were through with it? Why'd you let him pee on it?"

I can't help feeling a little smug about Zany's sweater getting peed on after all. If she'd stopped at the last exit, Haberdashery and I both could have gone to the bathroom.

"Do you have to be so crude?" I can't resist asking. "Can't you say he went to the restroom on it?"

Zany gets quiet then and doesn't speak for another half a mile, which is almost fifteen minutes, traffic-jam time.

chapter
6

"What's that?" I ask, poking a finger past Zany's elbow to stab at a bright red light on the dash.

"Oh, shoot," Zany mutters. "That means the car's too hot."

"Dang right it is," I agree, tugging at the neckline of my robe to let in a little air.

"I mean under the hood, Light Bulb."

"Oh." I peek toward the instrument panel again.

"You're the one that wanted the heat on," Zany accuses. I reach for the heat control and Zany slaps my hand away. "No, leave it on now. It'll pull some of the heat from the engine. When you overheat, you're supposed to keep the heat on and you're supposed to drive fast."

"Then thank goodness we're sitting in a traffic jam and going half a mile an hour. A hot engine doesn't sound like a good thing. What could happen if it gets too hot?" I ask Zany.

"It'll start snowing and a layer of ice will form," Zany gripes. "What do you think will happen if it gets too hot?"

So I'm picturing fire, but I'm too afraid to ask if that's what she means. Zany's like a bear when she realizes something's wrong, and what *isn't* wrong so far on this trip? By the time we make it the three miles to the rest area, both our faces look like red peppers from keeping the heat on full blast. When I creak my door open, the cold air hits and I start shivering. Haberdashery squeaks and hides himself under the backseat.

Zany's not only mad about the car. She keeps muttering about how, so far this trip, I've gotten her favorite sweater peed on and I've talked her ear off about how bad I have to use the toilet. It's a little weird how many of my failures, in Zany's eyes, involve bathroom emergencies.

"I don't know why I brought you," she growls, smacking the lock button and swinging the door shut. It's practically midnight and the rest area is mostly deserted. One old man walks a basset hound across a grassy hillside. The dog squats and I see Zany give him a dirty look. She must still be thinking about her sweater.

It's bright and clean inside the bathroom and the light wakes me up a little. I'm not used to being up so late. Mrs. Madison insists on bedtime at eight-thirty, and she overlooks the hour I spend reading under the covers. Tonight's book was a Nancy Drew mystery. Everything on Mrs. Madison's bookshelf is at least two decades old, and most of them were Mama Lacy's when she was little.

I feel better after I'm finished with the bathroom. I look at myself in the mirror, pink robe over yellow shirt, face starting to fade to a normal color. Zany is just now coming through the door. I know she stopped to smoke first. I can smell it in a cloud around her. She's rubbing her arms to warm up and I feel a tiny pang of guilt about her sweater. Her short white-blond hair is spikier than usual from being sweaty from the car's heat. I wonder if her damp hair will freeze out in the cold.

"Dang, Fella, you about laid rubber running in here at that speed." She wrinkles her nose in the direction of my feet. "Of course you couldn't lay rubber wearing nothing on your feet except one sock. Did you wash your hands?"

"Course," I lie. I'm not going to do it now that she's reminded me.

"Then go walk your dog." She hands me the car keys.

"How come? He already peed."

"I don't want him to do anything else in the car, is why." She slings her sweater into the sink and starts running water on it. I notice goose bumps on her bare arms. "I'm freezing."

"We're going south," I remind her. "It's supposed to get warmer."

"We're going southeast," she corrects. "That's not the same thing as going south. And it's still February and the middle of the night, even in Asheville." Her voice sounds different on the word *Asheville*. I think maybe she's missed it more than I have, since she remembers it better. Five years is long enough for me to have forgotten most of the details. I just remember feeling warm all the time there, even in February and the middle of the night.

I leave the bathroom. Outside it's darker and colder than I noticed on the way in. The basset hound man is gone and the only car is a canary-yellow Ford Ranger with a dented black passenger-side door and a rusty-looking topper over the bed. It belongs to a grumpy-looking guy with bangs that hang past his eyebrows. I feel a little scared, out here by myself with some guy. He heads toward the restrooms and I tense up as he passes me, but he turns his face away and doesn't slow down.

I head for our car and find that it's yipping. When I unlock the door, Haberdashery spins out like a tiny tornado.

"What, did you think we left you forever?" I ask the silly dog. He dashes up the hill into the darkness and stops to sniff where the basset hound was. After a long moment reassuring himself that the strange dog is gone, and a few moments spent covering the scent of the basset, I see him hunch up like he's got more business to do. I hate when Zany's right.

A door squeaks and I look toward the restrooms, hoping I'll see Zany. Instead it's the guy with the yellow truck, and he keeps glancing at me. I scoot away from him a little and watch him walk back to his truck, hoping he'll leave right away. But he lights a cigarette and leans against the tailgate. I start to fidget, hoping Zany finishes in the bathroom soon.

When I look away from the stranger, I realize the hillside in front of me is empty.

"Oh, shoot," I groan. Then I raise my voice. "Haberdashery? Where are you, stupid dog? Come here, you dumb thing!" I race after him, the dewy grass cold on my one bare foot. I hope the person with the basset hound followed the directions on the signs that say dog owners have to clean up after their pets. I would hate to wreck Mama Lacy's purple sock.

I'm almost over the hill when I hear Zany's raised voice behind me. "Fella? Ophelia, where'd you go?"

"Up here," I holler, waving an arm. I notice the stranger pointing after me with his cigarette, and I'm surprised, because this guy looks scary, but pointing me out to my sister is kind of a nice thing to do. I shout down to her, now that I've got her attention, "Haberdashery ran off! I've got to get him!"

"Why didn't you put him on a leash?" she shouts, but I ignore her and keep running. It wouldn't help to point out that she didn't give me time to find a leash. Behind me I hear Zany shout again, and I run a little faster. I'd like to have the dog caught and be on my way back before she catches up, so she can't get as mad at me. Also because if I have lost Mrs. Madison's poodle, I'm pretty sure I won't survive our homecoming tomorrow morning.

On the other side of the hill, white picnic tables stand out in the darkness, and the only light is from the moon. I see the poodle down past one of the tables, sniffing for scraps.

"Come on, stupid!" I jog toward the poodle, but he

stays out of reach. I lie on my stomach across the picnic table bench and hold my empty hand out toward Haberdashery, closed up in a fist so he can't tell I'm not holding anything. "Come here, ugly dog! Come on! Come see what I've got for you!"

He inches toward me, one paw at a time. He's almost close enough to grab when Zany catches up. She's panting, rubbing her arms in the cold.

"Shh, don't scare him!" I stretch out a little farther and wait for Haberdashery to take the bait. As he sniffs my empty hand, I snatch him into my arms by a handful of curly poodle hair. He squeaks but doesn't pull away.

"Thank goodness," Zany says. "Why did we bring that ugly thing?"

I gaze at her in amazement. "Because you wouldn't let me take him back!" The poodle is warm in my arms and I snuggle him a little closer. "We'd better get on the road. We're late, aren't we?"

Zany groans and follows me back to the car. I'm in and have my seat belt fastened before I notice my sister has stopped a few steps away.

"Come on!" I holler through my open door. "Are you coming or what?"

She turns in a complete circle and stops where she

started. "My purse is gone." Another circle, like maybe the purse will pop out of thin air and shout, "Surprise."

"What do you mean?" I ask dumbly.

"What do you think I mean, Fella? My purse is no longer here! That's what *gone* means!"

"Don't be stupid!" I hate when she talks to me like that, and I get madder. "Where'd you leave it?"

"On the hood of the car, Fella. I had to chase you down and I didn't want to lose you in the dark!" Her voice is high-pitched like after she chugs a Mountain Dew. "I mean, the money's not in it, but my wallet is. My driver's license, everything!"

"I'd have come back." I sulk. "You didn't have to leave your stupid purse lying around!"

"Help me look!" she demands.

I huff and heave and sigh, but I start her way to help, all the same. Halfway out of the car, I spot the change tub—or where the change tub used to be. I stop so quick my robe whispers and shimmers. My heart starts hammering.

"We've been robbed!"

She's still spinning in circles, scanning the grass. "Maybe it fell."

"I'm not talking about your purse, dummy!" I jump out of the car. "Zany, we got robbed! The change tub's gone!" I look at the empty parking spot where the smoker guy was leaning when I left to chase the dog.

She stops looking for the purse. "But that's where the gas money was!"

Then something else catches my eye—or, rather, doesn't. At once, I feel like I've swallowed a cold chunk of ice and it's freezing its way down through my stomach. I wrap my pink-robed arms around myself and grip my own elbows. Dread washes over me in waves so thick I have to work at not throwing up for a minute. "Oh, oh no. Oh no."

There must be something special in my voice, because Zany stops spinning and looks straight at me.

"What?"

"Ooooh." I can't find the words. Can't even wrap my brain around the thought. "Zany . . . ," I whisper. And, because that's not formal enough for the horrible thing that has happened, "Zoey Grace . . ."

She looks at me, waits. It has been at least six months since I've called her Zoey Grace. I see the thought cross her face, see her realize, an instant before I say it, what has happened.

"He stole Mama Lacy, too." I look back at my empty seat where I left the brass jar sitting. "Mama Lacy's gone."

chapter
7

The traffic jam is still clogging up I-77. Nobody's going anywhere quick, except for us. Zany swings the car onto the shoulder and blasts along at thirty miles an hour, which feels fast compared to all the stopped cars. The heat is back on and the red light is still burning on the instrument panel. I'm ready for fire, whether from the overheating engine or from a crash, I can't say. We're zipping up a steep hill and the earth drops away inches to my right. I squeeze Haberdashery with both arms and he sticks his cold nose under my armpit.

"We're not supposed to drive over here," I can't help but tell Zany.

"We're not supposed to leave the car unlocked, either." Her voice is a bit louder than mine, and I swallow the rest of my words. I'm not sure she could hear them very well, anyway. Our tires are riding on the bumpy strip of asphalt that's meant to wake sleepy motorists who have drifted onto the shoulder. The buzzing is so loud that Haberdashery keeps barking at it, his muzzle jerking against my arm. I'm trying to wedge my seat belt under him to put it on while Zany scans the stopped traffic for the thief. The canary-yellow pickup isn't hard to spot. Most of the traffic stuck on the interstate at this hour is big trucks pulling heavy loads. Zany hits the brakes so hard I bump my knees, and the dog, on the dashboard. She's out of the car before I can stop her, dodging through slow-moving traffic while I shout after her, "What are you going to do?" I'm scared to get out of the car, and scared to stay in the car alone. I'm pretty much scared to do anything at this point. I hear cars honking at my sister.

My heart starts thudding against the poodle I'm squeezing. What if the thief is dangerous? He sure looked dangerous when he was slouching next to his truck back at the rest stop. What if he does something bad to my sister? I've been without her for most of six months and even though I'm pretty sure she's nuts, the thought of losing her entirely has me flinging myself out of the car and into traffic. A big truck blares its horn and I scream and Haberdashery pees. I don't even have time to worry about the wet spot down my front. I shove Haberdashery back through the open window, afraid of dropping him in traffic. "Wait!" I tell him.

There shouldn't be so many cars on the interstate. It feels impossibly late to me, like midnight or after, but I know it can't be yet, because we haven't been driving that long. Everything looks bigger and scarier up close: the road, the cars, the tractor-trailers and the yellow truck Zany has just reached. By the time I catch up, she's got her arm through the driver's-side window of the robber's truck, and he's leaning back into the passenger seat to get away from her scrabbling fingers.

"Give it back!" Zany shrieks, and I see that she's totally lost it. That happens with Zany sometimes. She can shoot back sarcastic answers to my pestering nine times in a row, but on that tenth time, when she's had enough, she snaps. At this moment, she's going postal on the driver of the pickup truck. Up close, I can see he's not very old, maybe not even old enough to be smoking. He's trying to put his cigarette out in the ashtray so he can get both hands free to stop my sister from climbing through the window. He's just a kid, with six thousand freckles across his nose, and eyes that are too big for his face.

"Give it back!" Zany's yelling. "Real smart, stealing

from somebody during a traffic jam! Give it back right now! You don't even know what you took!"

"You don't even know what you're talking about." He starts cranking up his window, but Zany tosses herself through headfirst, preventing it from rolling up any farther. Her feet kick the side of the truck to give her more leverage so she can lift herself up. I notice the bottoms of her boots have her name written on them in glitter paint.

"What'd you think this was, a money jar?" she hollers, so I gather she's trying to get ahold of Mama Lacy's urn.

"People keep their money all kinds of weird places." He bumps his brake so my sister doesn't fall to her death. I want to balance her from behind, but there's nothing to grab except—well, her behind. I prop my shoulder under her hip instead, giving her what support I can.

"It isn't money!" Zany's voice comes out in a shriek. "Didn't you think to look? It's not money. It's my mother!"

There is a silent scuffle and Zany's body jerks away from me for a moment. Then she emerges from the truck window, urn in hand. I can see the thief's face, shadowed, in the truck, but I can't make out his expression. For several seconds, there is only the sound of car engines idling and the huff of all our breaths.

Then something yips.

Oh, crap.

I spin just as somebody's brakes give a squeak, and the yipping stops. Somehow I know what's happened even before I see Haberdashery lying still on the road, a car stopped in front of him with its doors hanging open.

Oh. Crap.

"Fella, wait!" Zany shouts, but I'm already darting back through the slow-moving traffic. I drop to my knees beside my grandmother's dog, and the driver who hit him, an old lady with her face all moon white, comes bustling up beside us.

"Is he dead?"

"Shut up, no he's not!" My voice comes out in a sob.

"What are you thinking, playing with a dog in traffic?"

"I wasn't playing, I was chasing ashes!" I don't care that what I'm saying makes no sense. I care that there is blood on Haberdashery's leg and he still isn't moving. I see him blink, and my breath comes out in a whoosh when I realize that he is alive. Still. He's clearly hurt and it's my fault and the guilt is enough to make me madder than I've ever felt.

"Traffic's going like two miles an hour. How could you not see a dog in front of your face?" I screech at the old lady.

"Fella!" Zany has caught up. To the driver, she says, "I'm sorry, ma'am. She's just worried about the dog."

The old lady is clutching her chest, mouth gaping open at my rudeness. Even though it isn't raining, she's wearing one of those see-through plastic covers that old ladies tie over their hair to keep it from melting.

"Let's get you back to the car," Zany says, tugging the old lady by the elbow. "Fella, get the dog and get out of the road. Let's go."

I'm scared to pick Haberdashery up and maybe break him worse, but it's not like we can stay here. Traffic's still trying to move in the other eastbound lane, and the gap in front of the old lady's car is growing longer.

With Haberdashery cradled in my arms, I start toward our car on the shoulder of the road, but two minutes later Zany turns me with her hands on my shoulders. She pushes me toward the thief's truck with its one black door standing out against all the yellow. "Get in."

"What?"

"Go."

I crane my neck in confusion, but our own car is hidden by the crush of slow-moving trucks. People keep honking at us, even though we're clearly trying our best to get out of the way. I'm still shaky with anger and upset. "Zany—"

"Go!" She shoves me, tugs me, steers me until she's gotten me into the truck with her and the thief. I'm wedged between my sister and the door handle, the injured poodle balanced on my knees.

"Go." This time she's talking to the driver.

"This ain't kidnapping, is it?" he asks. His freckles stand out against skin that's gone pale, and his hazel eyes are pinched behind round-lens glasses. I'm not sure whether he's worried that he's kidnapping us or that we're kidnapping him. For a thief, he's not very brave.

"Shut up. Look natural." Zany is at her bossiest in a crisis. She keeps her eyes straight ahead, so I immediately twist around to see what she's frightened of.

The driver who hit Haberdashery has started moving again and caught up with traffic. I peer backward toward Mama Shannon's car on the shoulder and I see what Zany's scared of. Flashing lights announce a police car, parked directly behind our car on the shoulder. A cop is peering in our window with his flashlight.

"Go back!" I shout. Even though Haberdashery can't usually stand me to be loud, he doesn't bark or even lift his head. "We can tell that cop we caught a thief, and he can help us get to a vet quicker!" I roll my window down. "Hey!" I shout toward the police car. "Hey! This guy's a thief! Hey!"

66

Then the stranger is tugging me back into the truck by my sleeve while my sister leans across me to close my window. "Shut *up*, Fella!" The truck swerves into the other lane and back again. The thief takes a couple of deep breaths in and swears as he steadies the truck.

"Why didn't you let me flag him down?" I demand as we inch out of sight of the police car. I can still see its blue lights flashing against the filthy backs of coal trucks. My heart sinks. "We've been robbed," I remind my sister.

Zany holds up the urn, which flashes red, catching the lights from the fire trucks and ambulances up ahead. An ambulance screams past us on the shoulder, and when its noise subsides, Zany says, "We can't go back. They'll send us home. The car's overheating, anyway. We couldn't have kept driving it. And did you forget? We're robbers, too, Fella."

The driver looks over with interest, but Zany glares and he turns to face the road.

"You can't stay in my car," he says. "I'm not harboring fugitives."

"We're not fugitives!" Zany protests. "We're just trying to get someplace!"

"Yeah, you and me both, and I can't get there if I'm getting arrested for kidnapping!"

"You should have thought of that before you broke into our car!" Zany sounds like she could spit nails.

"Didn't have to break in," the driver says. "You left it unlocked. Like a damn invitation. I just need to get there, and I'm almost out of gas, and you left your car unlocked. Fancy getup your sidekick there is wearing. I thought you probably had money."

I glance down at my shimmery robe and pajama pants and one bare foot. "Seriously?"

The robber cracks half a smile and then Zany cracks up laughing. My anger flares again.

"Quit it!" I shove Zany with the heel of my hand. "We've killed Haberdashery and you're laughing at my clothes!"

"Oh, stop being dramatic," Zany says, which she says to me lots, but I kind of feel like if there were ever a situation for dramatics, this would be it. We inch farther and farther from the police lights, drawing closer instead to the ambulance and fire truck lights up ahead. A fire-fighter waves us past the scene of a three-car accident. I can see crushed metal and shards of glass twinkling on the asphalt. I want very badly to crawl into the lap of either one of my mothers. Haberdashery is drooling in my arms, totally silent and still. I cradle him and wait.

chapter
8

We pick up speed on the open interstate
past the accident. It isn't till we're all the way back up to
seventy that Zany says, "This is what you get for robbing
strange cars, you know. Especially in a traffic jam, and in
a very noticeable yellow truck. You get two new passen-
gers with you, and an injured dog." She doesn't seem to remember that she and the thief were buddies just a second
ago, when it came to laughing at my outfit.

The driver clears his throat, tests his voice a couple
of times. "I didn't—I didn't know what I was stealing,"
he says after a minute. His voice is lower-pitched than
I would have thought for a guy so small and thin. He
sounds out of practice. "I wouldn't have stolen from y'all
if I knew."

"Well," Zany says, so matter-of-factly that she sounds like Mama Shannon, "we've done plenty of things wrong tonight, too. Now get off at the next exit. This dog needs a vet."

"I can't."

"You have to. It's your fault he got hit."

"No, I'm saying I can't. I have to be—I have to *get* there."

"You will. After this dog is taken care of. It's my grandmother's dog and my grandmother is already going to go ape when she finds out about all this and the least I can do is fix her stupid dog."

"I—" The boy huffs a sigh and swears.

"You don't want to be the one who killed this dog, do you?" Zany adds. "He's just a little dog. None of this is his fault!"

"Jesus! All right!" The kid has a lot of swearwords in his vocabulary, and he exercises most of them as he flips on his turn signal. I find it funny that a guy who would rob a fellow traveler at a rest stop would use his turn signal.

We pass two different hospitals and at least five doctor's offices before we finally find a vet. Even then, the windows are dark, the CLOSED sign just visible behind the glass. Of course. It's after midnight. I don't know how we're going to find a vet that's open at this hour, just aimlessly driving around some small Virginia town, peering at signs.

"You got a phone?" Zany asks the stranger. We were just about to pull out of the parking lot of the closed vet's office, and he hits the brakes. He feels around his pockets and produces a Nokia.

"Did you steal that?" I ask, and Zany shushes me.

"Call Information," she suggests. "Find a vet that's still open."

Instead, he passes the phone to Zany. She fights with it for a few seconds before placing her call.

"I can't—I don't—does anybody have something to write with?" She starts saying a phone number over and over, but it's different every time.

"Can't we find a phone book and look up a vet?" I suggest. Haberdashery's little leg is so hurt and he's not moving around very much, like maybe other things are hurt, too. I'm fighting back panic, but I don't know what I can do about it. I don't know how I ended up here, in the cab of some stranger's pickup truck with an injured dog and no vet and a plan all shot to pieces.

The driver doesn't answer, but he does swing us into a parking lot and pull over next to a pay phone.

"Well? Somebody go get the phone book," Zany says. She's handing the stranger back his phone, but she's looking at me. I can tell she's mad at me even though I'm not sure why.

"I don't want to move him," I say.

Zany huffs a short sigh. Then, "What's your name?"

"What do you mean, what's my name?"

"Not you." She jerks her head at the driver. "Him. What's your name? If I'm going to ask you to do stuff, I at least want to know who I'm asking."

"What kind of stuff are you going to ask me to do?"

"Stop at pay phones. Drive to vets. Tell me your name." She doesn't sound annoyed anymore. She sounds like something is a little bit funny. I can't imagine what.

"Adam."

"Pleasure," Zany says, and offers her hand. He looks at her strangely but takes one hand off the steering wheel to shake. He's peering at her through black wire-framed glasses that make his brown eyes seem too big for his face. Between the big eyes and the long hair that brushes down over them, he looks like some weird kind of puppy. I can't believe he ever struck me as scary. But Zany doesn't seem to agree. I've seen her gaze at other boys like this—Sam from her class and our old neighbor Garrett—but I've never seen a boy look back at her the same way. I get the weird feeling they've both forgotten I'm in the truck.

"Her name's Zany," I announce, "because she's completely crazy."

"My name is Zoey Grace," Zany corrects me. "The only people who call me Zany are completely crazy." She's not acting like herself at all. Usually she's proud of being Zany. "Adam. Will you do me a favor?"

"Depends." His accent sounds funny, different from any we would hear back home. I wonder how far he drove before he got to the rest area and stole from us.

"Will you please go check the phone book in that booth for a vet's office around here?"

"Emergency vet office," I add. "They have to be open twenty-four hours. Or at least at night."

"Don't know how we're going to pay a vet," Zany says, "but I guess we don't have much of a choice but to find one. Maybe they'll bill us."

"Or maybe we can call Mama Shannon and she can send us the money."

Zany twists all the way around in her seat to look at me, which is how I know I've said something wrong, only I don't know what it is.

"Maybe Mama Shannon can send us the money? To take Mrs. Madison's poodle to the vet?"

"Well, we're the ones who got him hurt."

"So? Mrs. Madison can afford it. Mrs. Madison can

73

afford a lot of things. Lawyers. Whatever she wants. She can afford a stupid vet for her stupid dog." Zany seems madder than she ought to, just for the bit of fight we seem to be having. One thing I'm noticing about Zany lately is that every little feeling she has gets blown up big.

The thought of calling Mrs. Madison is two hundred times scarier than the thought of calling Mama Shannon, who is my mother and has to love me no matter how bad I mess up. But I swallow, hard. Adam shifts uncomfortably in his seat. "I guess I can call Mrs. Madison if you want me to."

"No! Of course I don't want you to! I want you to be quiet a minute while I think!"

Adam's got the door half open already. "Let you all have a minute alone," he says, and heads toward the phone booth. I watch him flip through the pages, but I can't tell whether he's searching for vets or just stalling. Zany's staring after him, too, but I don't think she's really watching him.

"What a mess," Zany says, blowing out through her lips.

"It's not my fault." I'm quick to defend myself.

"God! I wasn't saying it was."

"But you think it is."

"No, shut up. Would you quit trying to pick a fight?"

"I'm not fighting. I'm just—" I huff a sigh. "Zany, maybe you really should have left me at home. All I've done is mess things up."

"Is that what you call that place?" Zany asks. "Home?" Too late, I realize I've messed up one more thing.

But I don't have anything else to call it. "Yeah. I mean, I live there. My stuff's there."

"Your stuff's there. What about your family?"

I suck in a breath and it comes out sounding like I'm crying, even though I'm not, exactly. "Zany, my family lives in a gross apartment with no room for me. And I live with somebody else. There's nothing I want to use the word *home* for." I huff another sigh. "Only it's hard to stop using words."

"Okay," she says after a minute.

Adam opens his door then, so we don't say anything else. He doesn't comment on the changed mood in the truck, even though I figure he's got to be able to tell.

"Did you find any vets?" Zany asks.

"There's an emergency clinic stays open twenty-four hours, according to their ad," he says, and hands Zany a sheet torn from the yellow pages.

75

The vet clinic turns out to be a small two-story building with a sign on the door urging patrons to call upstairs in case of emergency. There's no phone number, but Zany explains that they don't actually mean call. They mean I should climb the narrow metal staircase and knock on the door up top.

I hate being the one who has to do things. When we go out, Mrs. Madison always does the talking. Before that, back with my family, I always had a whole crowd of people who could do the talking for me. It's not that I'm shy. I just don't see the point in being the one to place an order with a waitress, ask for directions, or tell the librarian I need to renew my books when there are other, much more loudmouthed people around.

But this is my grandmother's dog and I'm the one who brought him. Tucking him into my robe, I hurry up the stairs. It looks like an apartment, like maybe the vet lives above her little clinic. She has a sticker on her window that says IN CASE OF FIRE, with a list of names of pets to rescue, all named for things out of the sky: Cloudy. Starry. Sunshine. Through the little window in the door, I can see a green microwave clock glowing in a kitchen. It says 12:41 and I groan. We're supposed to be more than halfway to Asheville by now. I'm pretty sure we haven't even made it a fourth of the way.

It's hard to knock with an injured poodle in your arms. I end up bumping the door awkwardly with my knee. "Hey . . . Hello in there? My dog needs help! Hello?"

The apartment stays dark and silent and I'm pretty sure nobody's home. Maybe the vet got called out on another emergency. Maybe somebody else's dog got hit by a car tonight, or maybe the people in that three-car accident had a dog with them and it got hurt.

Then I hear creaking inside the apartment, and I take a step back and cradle Haberdashery so tightly, he gives a little squeak.

I hear locks sliding and then the door swings open and I'm looking into the blinking face of a skinny old woman with gray hair down past her butt. Cats are circling her ankles like moths circle a candle. Occasionally, without glancing down, she stomps her foot in front of one of them to keep it from escaping. She's wearing a lumpy robe with cat hair all over it, pockets bulging with who knows what, like maybe sardines or something.

"What have we here?" she says.

I'm too scared to speak, so I shove the poodle at her.

"Sweet boy," the vet croons at my grandmother's dog, gathering him into her arms, and then I feel at ease enough to speak, because she doesn't sound nearly as stern as she looks, although her cats are hissing and growling at Haberdashery. I have trouble believing they've got names like Cloudy and Sunshine.

"He got hit by a car," I say. Then I add, hopefully, "But it was going real slow."

She peers past me at the yellow truck waiting in the parking lot. "You got parents with you, young lady?"

"Just my sister and—and her boyfriend." I'm sure if I say we've accepted a ride from a dead-mother thief who got caught red-handed, she'll call the police. "We were coming back from a late movie and the poodle got out and there was a car—" It's all jumbled and I hope she chalks it up to me being worried and sleepy, not to me telling a whopper of a lie.

"Well." The vet shakes her head slowly. "He doesn't look too bad off, really. Meet me downstairs. I'm going to get some clothes on." She eases the dog back into my arms.

I hurry back down the steps, glad to put some distance between me and those evil-looking cats. I see Zany leaning out the passenger window.

"What's going on?" she mouths.

"She's coming downstairs," I whisper, like maybe if she hears me, she'll change her mind.

The vet unlocks the clinic from the inside and I carry

Haberdashery through the doors. She switches on lights here and there as she leads me down a long hallway. I've never seen a vet's office after dark, and it looks spooky. I think about the animals who might have died here and wonder if cats and dogs have ghosts.

"I'm Dr. Tarnish," the vet says, opening the door to an exam room. "Put him on the table there. What did you say your name was?"

"Dr. Tarnish? What kind of a name is that?"

"The kind of name that belongs to a vet who'll get up in the middle of the night to see to your dog." She fixes me with a stare and does not forget her question. "Your name, young lady?"

"Ophelia." It doesn't occur to me to lie, and I skip my nickname because people look at me strangely when I say "Fella," since I'm a girl and all.

"Pretty name."

"My Mama Shannon gave it to me after one of her favorite songs." It's been a long time since me and Mama Shannon danced around together, singing my namesake song. My heart hurts.

"And the dog?"

"Haberdashery."

Her eyebrows disappear under her gray bangs. "Well, that's a new one!"

"My grandmother keeps him all clipped and proper and sometimes she puts a bow tie on him, so my grandfather used to call him Haberdashery because that's a fancy clothes store for men and he looked like a well-dressed gentleman. The poodle, I mean, not my grandfather. From what I remember, *he* had crazy hair and always wore flannel." Weirdly, talking about the Madisons makes me miss my grandmother, even though I saw her earlier this evening. I don't miss her the way I do Mama Lacy or Mama Shannon or even Zany. I miss her different. But I do miss her, and it surprises me. I thought I hated her, but can you miss people you hate?

"I see." Dr. Tarnish is peering into Haberdashery's eyes with a light, feeling his legs, squeezing his stomach. She turns on some clippers and buzzes a spot of hair off his leg, then dabs on red medicine and wraps the paw in gauze.

"Good as new," she says, patting the dog and giving me a smile.

It can't be that simple. But Haberdashery, dazed though he is, doesn't seem to be bleeding anymore, and his breathing seems normal.

"Really? You mean he didn't break anything? 'Cause he didn't get up for a few minutes and I thought maybe he broke something." I can hear my own voice shaking.

The idea of coming home with a broken poodle is frightening.

"Probably stunned him, is all." She picks him up gently and looks him in the eye. "Now you stay out of trouble, old fellow," she says, and hands him to me. I tuck him against my now-bloody pink robe and I see Dr. Tarnish looking.

"Odd thing to wear to the movies," she comments.

"Well, it was a late movie," I remind her. "I'm going to go put him in the car. Um, how much . . . I mean . . ."

"Receptionist doesn't come in till nine. Leave your parents' information and I'll have him contact you with the bill."

I have no idea what information I'm supposed to leave. If I write down Mrs. Madison's phone number, or Mama Shannon's for that matter, will Dr. Tarnish call one of them right now? But she said the receptionist wouldn't be in until nine, so it'll probably be at least that late before a call is made. I glance out toward the truck while I'm stalling, and I'm distracted by Zany, who is waving from the window.

"Here's the form," the doctor says. "You don't have to fill it all out. Just leave your parents' name, phone number, and address. When James contacts you, he can put your parents' information in the computer."

Zany and Adam are both going nuts outside in the truck. I see arms waving. I scribble down Mama Shannon's information. She's really my parent, after all. "Yes, ma'am. I mean, doctor. I mean—I mean, thank you."

I jog toward the truck because I can't imagine what's going on, but I can tell it's not good. By the time I reach it, Zany's got the door open, and she pulls me and Haberdashery inside. Adam barely waits for the door to close before he hits the gas.

"What's going—oof!" The truck peels out of the parking lot so quickly I fall against the door, Zany smushing me from the middle.

"You're missing," Zany says, and turns up the radio.

chapter
9

"*. . .* **was reported missing shortly** *after midnight by her custodial grandmother. Ophelia Madison-Culvert is four feet nine inches tall and was last seen wearing a pink satin bathrobe.*"

It's incredibly weird to hear myself talked about on the radio.

"Not the best outfit to run away in," Adam says, eyeing my robe.

"She's pretty bad at running away in general," Zany says.

"Am not! I'm just doing what you tell me!"

Zany starts listing the ways in which I've failed already tonight. "You brought the stupid dog. You didn't lock the car at the rest stop. You didn't roll up the window so the dog couldn't get out on the interstate. You *gave the dog my sweater*. You have absolutely been a *treat* this trip, Ophelia!"

"Shut up, you haven't done so great, either! You're the one who left your purse on the hood of the car. You're the one who forgot the camera and put us way behind! You're the one who wanted to go on this stupid trip in the first place! You're the one who stole Mama Lacy off the mantel!" I see Adam look at her and then back at the road.

"Do not blame this on me," Zany says in this voice like she knows there's a chance it's her fault. "I couldn't have known what would happen. Shoot, I *still* don't know what's going to happen."

This is the point in the argument where we would ordinarily storm off in opposite directions, but we're cooped up in the cab of a truck. Her hand reaches over once in a while to stroke the poodle. Mine reaches toward her now and then to touch the urn.

I figure Zany's mad enough that she's got to let off steam somehow, because she whips around quickly to fix her gaze on Adam. "And *you*."

"What?"

"What do you mean, *what*? Stealing my mother's ashes? Stealing our gas money, which you still haven't given back, by the way."

"We're using my gas," Adam says.

"That's not the point. The point is—the point is—"

"The point is you stole from us," I offer. "We were already having what Mama Lacy calls 'an impossible go,' and then you stole from us and made it even worse."

"And look where it got me," Adam says. "Way off course and way off schedule. I ought to have driven right on past you in that traffic jam."

"She didn't give you much choice, if I remember," I say.

"Well, it don't matter. I've got to make up time." The truck moves a little faster as he says it. "I need to get there."

"Get where? Where's so important you got to get to that you'd rob two kids at a rest stop when they're just looking for their dog?"

Adam wraps and rewraps his fingers around the steering wheel. He's quiet for more than half a mile before he answers.

"My dad," he says in this awful voice I recognize. I see him glance over at the urn.

Zany asks, quiet, "What's the matter with your dad?"

Adam changes lanes and accelerates. I already know what he's about to say, because the air in the truck disappears to make room for the word.

"Cancer," he says, soft as rain. In school I learned about onomatopoeia, words that sound like what they are. *Crash. Splash. Pop. Sizzle.* I think *cancer* is one of those words. Something that sounds soft and simple, but it latches on and grows, and when somebody says it once, everybody starts saying it again and again, a cancer of vocabulary, a word that won't stop growing.

I don't say anything, but after a minute I reach over and take the urn from Zany. It's warm from her grip. I hold it against my chest, careful not to bump Haberdashery, and I rock it gently, trying to do for Mama Lacy what she used to do for me.

"Where's your dad?" Zany asks.

"Wytheville," he says. "I can take you that far, but then I'll have to stop. You need to find another way from there."

I close my eyes and try to picture the map, which is still sticking out of the glove box of our car back on the shoulder of I-77. I'm not sure exactly where Wytheville is, but I know it's a long way from Asheville. I think maybe this will be when Zany decides we should go back to the car. It would be cool by now. It would be safe to drive again—to drive right back home to West Virginia and forget this night ever happened.

But the thought doesn't seem to cross Zany's mind.

"That's what we're good at," she says, quiet, reaching to take the urn back from me. "Finding another way." She sounds so sad, I don't answer. I don't know where she gets that, though. I thought what we were good at was losing things, not finding them.

chapter
10

"It's Sunday," Zany announces after a while. I glance at the clock and she's right. It's close to one in the morning, so it's Sunday, and it's February 29, a day that only comes once every four years. Everything was so different last time it was February 29.

Sundays are the hardest days since Mama Lacy died. I go to church with Mama Shannon and Zany and there's the loneliness of the empty seat next to us. No one's ever filled Mama Lacy's seat and everybody talks *at* us, but nobody really talks *with* us. They mean well, they just don't know us. We only went to church in the first place because Mama Lacy wanted us to, and it took us a few churches to settle on one, and mostly the one we settled on, we picked because it was busy and we didn't have to really *know* anybody. We get squeezes and hair pats and handshakes and kisses, everybody tripping over themselves to be sure everyone can tell *those people* are welcomed in this church—that *that family* isn't being excluded because of their *preferences*. Their words these days are all the same: "Take care, now." "Take care of each other." "Take care of you." A reminder, over and over again, that our best caretaker is gone.

I don't like to listen to the "she's with Jesus" stuff, either. Maybe it's wrong, but I don't like to think about Mama Lacy being with Jesus, who I've never met, when she ought to be with me, her daughter. Somehow I can't picture her in a white robe and angel wings when she's supposed to wear denim skirts and dress flats.

So I tune out the *take care*s and I tune out the Jesus stuff, and that doesn't leave a whole lot of church to care about. Mostly I study Mama Shannon's face, which only looks familiar in certain light. I don't think it's fair that the one day of the week we get to spend together, we spend in a place where we can't talk.

Me and Mama Shannon used to talk a lot. She liked to get up early and so did I, and that meant lots of early-morning conversations while Zany and Mama Lacy were still sleeping. She would let me sip her coffee, which didn't taste good at first, but I wanted to make her proud, so I kept trying. I would ask her the questions that had been on my mind that week, like, "Can bugs see germs, since they're both so little?" And, "Why can't we get another cat?" And, "What if Mama Lacy doesn't get better?" And she would ask me the questions that had been on her mind that week, like, "What should I do with my hair?" And, "How many cats do you think one family needs?" And, "Should we go back to Asheville?" And, "What if Mama Lacy doesn't get better?" She never talked to me like I was a kid. We were just two Madison-Culvert women chatting over coffee.

Now we haven't talked in six months.

Not *about* anything. When Mama Shannon picks me up from Mrs. Madison's, she quizzes me on whether I'm fed and sleeping and passing my classes, and then she goes quiet, not the sad, about-to-cry quiet of the first few weeks after Mama Lacy, but more of an awkward silence, like she's not sure what to say. Usually, she ends up mumbling about whatever's around us. "When did they close the dollar store?" "Fancy cars they've got on this street." "Funny-looking dog." Sometimes I remember our conversations and our questions for each other, and I think, *This. This is what happens if Mama Lacy doesn't get better. We all come apart.*

When we get back to Mrs. Madison's after church

each week, I always ask Mama Shannon to come in and she always says no. She never so much as looks at the house, knuckles white on the steering wheel, eyes on me or on the road. Zany does, though. Sometimes I catch her staring. I can't tell whether it's at the long, paved driveway or the wrought-iron patio railings or the little frosted windows on each side of the door, but she stares. Sometimes I can see the bitterness and longing all mixed up on her face before she and Mama Shannon drive away. Zany's eyes are so expressive. You can see so much in them, frowns and tears and smiles, even though the feelings hardly ever reach the rest of her face these days.

Mrs. Madison doesn't come in to chat at bedtime on Sundays. She seems to realize I want my space.

The rest of the week, she tries to be friendly. Offers me something to drink or brings me chocolate chip cookies or something grandmotherly like that. It doesn't fit with how she looks, pointed shoes and dyed-blond hair. She doesn't seem the chocolate chip type.

Usually when she tries to make friends with me like that, I pout and hide and refuse to speak to her, and eventually she goes away.

Then I start feeling bad. Remembering how when I was six and broke my pinkie, she brought me a teddy bear at the doctor's office. Reminding myself of the picture of me she keeps on her nightstand, taken when I was seven or so, when Mama Lacy was better for a while. That happens sometimes, with cancer. You get better, and you stay better for a while—even for years—and then all of a sudden, you're not better anymore. In that middle part, when Mama Lacy was feeling good and liked to visit, I used to go with her to see Mrs. Madison a lot—back when I was still little enough to call her Grandma—and we'd eat the fancy butter cookies that were supposed to be dipped in tea, except I didn't like tea back then, so I crunched through them one painful bite at a time to be nice to my grandma. I think about how she remembered that, remembered it enough to buy me chocolate chip cookies this time around.

So then, feeling bad, I'll go to find her, and by then she's upset and she won't say more than a couple of words to me. I feel like if things were normal, if Mama Lacy were still alive and I was only staying at Mrs. Madison's as a visitor, we could be friends. She's a strange, formal old lady and she panics at the smallest things, like when the refrigerator makes a noise and she thinks it's going to catch on fire, or when the FedEx lady knocks on the door and she thinks it's the IRS come to take her house because "they can just do that, you know." She's suspicious of everybody and afraid of almost everything.

I feel like I'm a lot of things to Mrs. Madison—a distraction when she's trying to read a romance novel, a bother when I knock things over in the kitchen, and a nuisance when she's sipping wine with her friends from the gardening club, which hasn't gardened in years. But I also think that sometimes, just once in a while, when she's nervous at night and she doesn't like to be alone, she's glad I'm there.

To be honest, I feel the same way. Mrs. Madison bothers me because she's not Mama Shannon . . . or Mama Lacy. But she tries really hard to do nice things for me, and most of the time, I'm glad I have her.

It's still sixteen miles to Wytheville and I'm preoccupied with trying to shield me and Haberdashery with my robe to save us from the secondhand smoke coming from my two fellow travelers, when Adam pulls the truck into the mostly empty parking lot of a grocery store.

"What are we doing?" I ask.

"Refueling," Adam says, which doesn't make any sense because there aren't any gas pumps. The only thing in the parking lot besides us is a pink convertible. The sign on the door says CLOSED, but the lights are still on.

"What grocery store pays well enough you can drive

a pink convertible to work?" Zany wonders. She worked all last summer at Face Facts Beauty Supply, selling cosmetics to help get by when Mama Shannon's grocery store job wasn't enough to pay for Mama Lacy's medical costs, plus groceries and rent. She's been mumbling ever since about salaries, about how nobody can be expected to earn a living at these wages. She sounds more like Mama Shannon every day.

Adam's not paying attention. Instead he's pulled up sort of near the pink convertible. Near enough to the pink convertible that I realize his plan almost as soon as he's out of the truck.

"Zany, is he—is he stealing from that person?"

She glances out. Watches Adam as he sticks his arm through the half-rolled-down window and starts trying to hit the lock. Two tries. Three. The door opens.

She says a word she's not supposed to say in front of me.

"Quick, drive away before he steals! If we're here when he does it, we'll be accomplices! They send you to jail for that!" I'm still certain this trip is going to end with us in jail.

Zany's staring at me now, forgetting to keep an eye on our car-burgling companion. "And if we steal his truck, we're criminals instead of accomplices. You know they send you to jail for *that*, too."

Oh. Right. "I forgot we're not in Mama Shannon's car."

"Yeah, because a blue Subaru Forester and a canary-yellow Ford Ranger with a black passenger door are easy to mix up."

"Shut up." I wish I had another inch of elbow room for every time my sister and I have said *shut up* to each other on a car trip. We've done pretty well this time, but I can't help but say it now.

We turn back to Adam, who is sitting slyly in the pink car, going through things. I want to get out and tell him to stop, but I feel tongue-tied, which is what happens when I have something really important to say. Slowly, I ease the passenger door open and step out of the truck. Zany's on my heels, dangling Adam's car keys. She pushes me behind her and moves ahead of me. Relief, and a little disappointment to have chickened out, washes through me. Zany's going to take care of this, so I don't have to.

I climb back into the truck, where it isn't quite as cold. In the store, I can see a black ponytail bobbing up and down the aisles. She doesn't look like the type to leave money in her car, but then, Zany and me probably don't, either, and we made the same mistake.

Zany is dragging Adam back to the truck by his elbow. I let her in and wait for the motor to roar to life, but though we're all inside, nothing happens except that Adam feels around the steering wheel, the dashboard, and the seat for a minute. Then he says, "Where the hell are my keys?"

"In my pocket," Zany announces, "and they'll stay there until you put back what you took."

Adam stares straight ahead for a minute. His jaw is set, stubborn, and his eyes look tired.

"Look, lady—" he begins.

I can't help but giggle. I've never heard anybody call my sister "lady" before.

Zany nudges me silent and holds her ground with Adam, whose face is going darker with each word.

"My dad's sick," he says. "We don't have no gas money. We're going to run empty by the next exit. What do you want from me?"

"I want you to go put that money in that car before I call the police."

"You ain't got a phone." Because he sure isn't going to give us his.

"Bet that store does." She holds up the keys. "You

want these, you'll go put that money back where you got it. Now."

He doesn't move. "We're not getting far without money."

"What happened to our gas money?" Zany asks. "You know, that you stole out of our car when you stole—"

He waves her off. "I know what I stole. Okay? And I'm not taking y'all's money. You're going to need it to get where you're going."

The mention of our gas money makes me remember that I have money with me, too. I'm scared to say anything, and my voice comes out in a squeak. "I got money."

Zany turns slowly from Adam to me. "What are you talking about?"

"I . . . got money," I repeat. I reach into my purple sock and take out a soggy twenty.

Zany stares and stares. "You've got twenty bucks and you didn't say anything?"

"It's not mine. It's Mrs. Madison's. She makes me keep it in my sock in case of emergencies."

"She makes you keep twenty dollars in your sock? Even at bedtime?"

I can hear my voice getting louder. "She's afraid I'll get lost or kidnapped or separated from her and I'll need money for a taxi or a phone or food or something. Or if the river floods and we have to run away really quick. Or if robbers break in and everything we owned was stolen. She says at least this way we'll have forty bucks to get us started again."

"Forty? You mean Mrs. Madison keeps twenty bucks in her sock, too?"

"No, she keeps hers . . ." I blush. "Somewhere else." I cross my arms over my chest. I'm not about to say *bra* in front of Adam.

Adam lets out a breath and it sounds so weird that for a minute, I think he's crying. Then I realize he's actually laughing. Zany notices at the same time and we both turn on him.

"And what's so funny?"

"You two are just . . . you're just like a sitcom. You should have a laugh track."

"Shut up. Are you going to put the money back? Since it sounds like we have enough already?" She looks sideways at me.

He shakes his head. "Fine. But if I get caught putting the money back, it's on y'all. It's always when the thief goes back that he gets caught." Zany looks pointedly at me when he says this, like having Adam say it makes it true.

While he's gone, she keeps looking at me, but the look changes from "so there" to something more serious.

"It's a different world over there at Mrs. Madison's, isn't it?"

I shrug. Something about her stare makes me uncomfortable. It annoys me how she can stay so calm sometimes, even when she's mad, if there's a point to make. "I don't know. Why?"

"You had twenty bucks in your sock and you forgot about it till now?"

"I didn't forget. It just wasn't an emergency."

She stares at me. Keeps staring till I squirm. She's about to speak, but then Adam gets in the truck and Zany doesn't say anything else, which isn't like her.

All the way back onto the interstate, I chew the inside of my cheek. I know money's tight with Mama Shannon and Zany. But I've been with Mrs. Madison for six months, and Mrs. Madison can blow twenty bucks on potpourri at the Family Dollar. So I wasn't thinking about twenty dollars being a lot of money. I wasn't thinking about it being money at all. It was just another of Mrs. Madison's goofy habits.

Now that I see the hurt expression on Zany's face, I'm trying to add up how many hours she would have to work at Face Facts to earn twenty dollars. I'm trying to count how many boxes of butter noodles twenty dollars could buy. I'm thinking about the chicken I had for dinner last night and my nightly mug of hot chocolate before bed, and I'm feeling sick. How could I forget twenty dollars was a lot? Guilt chews at me. If I could have a coffee conversation with Mama Shannon tomorrow, that would be the first question I asked her. But I can't. I think maybe those days are gone for good, and the thought makes my voice clog up with sadness.

"I didn't forget," I say thickly.

"Okay," Zany says.

"I didn't."

"Okay."

We don't talk anymore for a while.

chapter
11

I doze off and wake up feeling like hours have passed, but the dash clock says it was only fifteen minutes. For a second, I'm not sure where I am, or why the dash clock is in the wrong place, or what the warm thing is that's asleep on my knees.

"You missed the exit!"

Oh. Zany. Adam. Truck. Haberdashery. Right.

"That was Wytheville!" Zany slaps at Adam in a way that startles me. It's a playful slap, not exactly like she'd play with me, but not angry. "That was our turn. What were you looking at?"

As I clear the cobwebs from my brain, I can guess what he was looking at instead of the road. He glances at Zany and then away, and though I wouldn't expect to see a street thief blush, there it is in front of me.

Flashing arrows announce a steep curve in the road and we swing around it too fast. I grab at Haberdashery to keep him from falling onto his injured leg. He wags his nubby tail and licks my hand once in thanks, which is the friendliest Haberdashery has ever been with me.

"Get off here," Zany says, pointing at the next exit. "It says Wytheville, too. We can still get where we're going."

Adam does as he's told. I hope the truck drivers are paying attention, because he doesn't signal this time before darting toward the off-ramp.

The first thing we see is a gas station, which is good because I need to pee really bad.

"Stop," I beg. I don't have to say why. Zany guesses.

"Again?" she wails. "We were just at a gas station twenty minutes ago! Why didn't you go then?"

"I didn't have to go then!"

"Fella! Your bladder's the size of a pen cap! This trip's going to take for*ever*!"

"If Adam wants his truck to stay dry—" I warn.

"It's an old truck," Adam says, but he pulls into the gas station anyway and I shove the door open as soon as we've stopped.

"Two seconds," I shout over my shoulder.

"One . . . ," Zany hollers after me. As the door swings shut, I hear, "Two!"

I have to go into the gas station to get the bathroom key, and I'm terrified they're going to recognize me from my description on the radio. I keep my head down, chin pressed almost to my chest, as I mumble about needing the key. The cashier's wearing a blue polo shirt with coffee stains on it, but I don't know what her face looks like, because she never looks up. I'm convinced I can hear my heart pounding as I scurry away, key in hand.

The light in the restroom is flickery, and there are things like phone numbers and crude words on the walls. In the cracked mirror, I study how different I already look from the way I looked when I last saw my reflection, back at the rest area where we first crossed paths with Adam. *That* mirror was clean and whole, and I was clean, too, though I haven't felt whole in a while. I've got blood on my pink robe from the poodle's injured leg, and I'm all rumpled and wrinkled, and even though I can't see it on me, I know I smell like dog pee and cigarette smoke.

I wonder what Mama Lacy would think if she could see me. Mama Lacy, who carried Wet-Naps and hand sanitizer in her purse. Mama Lacy's purse was like a magic trick, twice as big on the inside as it looked on the outside. Inside, she kept one of each of everything you could possibly need. Now it, like her, is gone forever, emptied and given away—or thrown away—a piece at a time by Mrs. Madison. No more Wet-Naps and hand sanitizer. No more Tic Tacs and Trident gum, no more safety pins, spare buttons, and the menus to every fast-food place we might ever need to order from. I gaze at the sad girl in the mirror for a minute longer, but even her hair doesn't look familiar, tangled as it is. I think Mama Lacy might not even recognize me if she happens to peek down from heaven.

Three steps out of the station, I stop next to the gas pumps. My bare left foot feels slimy from the concrete, and I'm freezing. The truck is still running, puffing out blue exhaust. In the front seat, Adam is kissing my sister.

I can feel my heart beat now all the way in my stomach. My face crinkles up and I have to work at smoothing it. Only when I can draw a breath without letting it out in a screech do I climb back into the cab of the truck. I slump against the window, forehead flat on the cold glass.

"Ready?" Zany asks cheerfully. She doesn't seem to know that I saw them kissing. She also doesn't seem concerned about whether I'm ready or not. Adam pulls onto the road while I'm still fighting with Haberdashery to get an inch of freedom to fasten my seat belt, and we wind our way in the direction that Zany thinks might be toward Wytheville.

"That sign said go right," I say when Adam stays on the main road instead of turning where the sign told him.

"That sign doesn't know what it's talking about," Adam answers.

"But—but that sign said go right." My voice goes a little higher. I'm starting to feel sort of scared, like maybe I really am being kidnapped or something. All those scary movies about kids being kidnapped, which I'm now furious at Zany for letting me watch, start with the kid accepting a ride from a stranger. And then the stranger doesn't go where he's supposed to, he drives off on some little two-lane road, and the whole thing ends in a scary cabin with a humongous ransom demand.

"Adam, I swear, that was where we were supposed to go," Zany says, and I detect a hint of uneasiness in her voice, too. I scoot closer to her again.

Adam shakes his head and keeps driving. Just when I'm trying to figure out how to be sneaky about opening my window so I can scream, Adam says in this little-boy voice, "I'm not ready yet."

Oh, shoot. That.

"I'm not—I mean, I know this is it, and I don't know—I haven't figured out what to—" He's stuttering worse than Zany when she's had four Mountain Dews. A few tenths of a mile slip by.

"What to say," Zany prompts.

"Yeah."

"Christ, I still haven't figured out what to say." Where Adam's voice got younger, Zany's sounds older. Old as Mrs. Madison.

I remember wondering what to say, too. Remember what it felt like, walking down the cold hospital hallway, knowing to my bones it was the final visit, even though I was only eleven and nobody would tell me anything for sure. I remember taking so long in the hallway that by the time I was ready to enter the room, it was too late. It was over too quick, and nothing felt final.

Zany must be thinking of the same awful day, because she's got her hand on Adam's shoulder and she doesn't even care if I see.

"This feeling's not going to go away," she says, rubbing the brass container with her other hand. "But take all the time you need."

I knew she would say that, but it still makes me groan. Taking all the time Adam needs means derailing our own trip even further. But I've been through what

Adam's going through, and I can't seem to say a word. Can't seem to stop wishing I could trade places with him and be back where he is now. Maybe then I could find the right words at the end. Maybe then I could say good-bye properly.

That was supposed to be what the memorial was for—to say good-bye, in case you hadn't already. But at the memorial, the lights were too dim and the flowers smelled too strong and the picture of Mama Lacy didn't even look like her, really. And there we all were, clumped together, none of us sure what to say. We were a bunch of strangers who were supposed to be family. I remember recognizing maybe half of the relatives gathered. I remember Mrs. Madison in her ridiculous hat, and I elbowed Zany but neither of us laughed.

It was supposed to be the final good-bye, but good-byes should be said with hugs and *see you laters*, not awkward silences among strangers and a smiling, still photo at the front of the room. Family drifted into groups, then away toward the doors. Nothing felt final.

I've been waiting ever since for another chance, but it hasn't come yet.

chapter
12

"Let me show you what you do to get your mind off things," Zany says, and she reaches across me to open the passenger door. "Move, Light Bulb!" Without waiting for me to do it, she slides across me, stepping on my toes and shoving Haberdashery more firmly down into my lap. He lets out a low growl and I rub behind his ears to quiet him. Zany runs around the front of the truck, flashing in and out of the headlights. Adam's pulled over to find his lighter, which fell off the seat and under the gas pedal, and he doesn't protest when Zany nudges him over into the middle spot and slides in behind the wheel.

Adam takes up a different amount of space than my sister, and he's a different shape and temperature.

I squeeze myself against the door as tight as I can, but there's no avoiding touching him.

"Am I squashing you?" he asks when I keep fidgeting. I shake my head wordlessly. I feel my cheeks getting pink. I'm not used to sitting so close to a boy, especially one who was recently kissing my sister.

Zany's loving the truck. She revs it more than necessary and goes a little faster than the speed limit says. I'm startled when she swings us into a department store, both because we don't have any extra money and because I can't imagine what she needs to buy at this hour. It's one of those huge twenty-four-hour stores with a grocery section and a restaurant and a bank inside. There are hardly any cars in the parking lot.

Zany parks near the doors and tugs at Adam till he follows her. They walk hand in hand, and I sulk a few paces behind, jealous. I haven't had my sister to myself for six months and I want her attention. But she's distracted by this sad thief we've found, who's stuck six months behind us in the process of something awful.

We make it three steps into the store before a cashier says, "Young lady!"

My heart thumps up into my throat. *Oh no*, I think, *she's recognized us from the news!* I immediately start looking around for police officers, or at least security guards. But all the cashier says is, "You can't be in here without shoes."

"Oh." I glance down, heart hammering. I'm so used to parading around in one soaking-wet sock, I'd forgotten it isn't normal.

"Way to act natural, walking around without shoes," Zany says. "Geez, wait here." She darts away. I see her going through the checkout a minute later, and she comes back with a pair of yellow canvas sneakers with an orange clearance sticker on them. I don't want to take off Mama Lacy's sock, so I wear one shoe with a sock and one shoe without.

Zany grabs a cart and I realize why we're here. She does this every time she gets stressed. It's the most ridiculous way of letting off steam I've ever witnessed, but for some reason, being a jerk always makes Zany feel better. She leads us from aisle to aisle, piling the weirdest things into the cart. Cushioned insoles. Feminine hygiene products. Cat litter. Chocolate bars.

"Come on, Adam, help me!" she says, and insists that he choose something silly off the shelves to add to the cart. "Pick something crazy that nobody in their right mind would buy." She seems to approve when he chooses a giant jar of olives.

"Are you going to play, Fella?" Zany asks over her

110

shoulder. I shake my head and slump along after her, still pouting. My sneakers are squeaking and my left one, the one with no sock, keeps slipping around out of place.

We make it to the electronics section with Zany shrieking, "Headphones! Twelve pairs of headphones, and nothing to plug them into!" Adam's not exactly smiling yet, but his face has softened and I think I see his eyes get brighter. It's hard not to laugh at how amused my sister is by her goofy additions to the shopping cart. Even I'm starting to smile—until my gaze lands on the digital camera section and I feel all of a sudden like I've lost something. I check both robe pockets and my sock before I realize what it is.

"Mama Lacy's camera!" My wail is a little loud for the middle of the night in a nearly empty store. I see a stock guy glance at us and I lower my voice. "I forgot it!"

"What?" Zany's distracted, trying to decide between earbuds and noise-canceling.

"I left—I left Mama Lacy's camera in Mama Shannon's car."

Now I've got my sister's full attention. She shakes her head once. "No, you didn't. It's in my purse," she says, not looking at all certain. She feels for her purse, but she's left it in the truck. I see her hand lift to her hair. I know she's remembering, like I'm remembering, how she brushed her hair as soon as we got in the truck with Adam, how her purse was light and empty and she didn't have to dig under anything as cumbersome as a camera to get at her hairbrush. I watch her face fall. "Fella—"

"It's not my fault!" I interrupt. "You're the one that went back for the camera in the first place. You should have remembered it!"

"I was a little busy stealing our dead mother's ashes back from a thief!" She pats Adam's elbow as she says this, as if to show there are no hard feelings.

"Well, I was trying to rescue my grandmother's poodle from certain death! Which I wouldn't have had to do anyway if you'd let me take him back when he first got out and followed us! You blame me for everything!"

She begins chucking packages of earbuds into the cart with alarming force. "We're not playing the blame game, Fella. I just don't understand why you can't ever think about things. It's not like we didn't stop at home to get the camera. It's not like we didn't tiptoe through the house. And then you got it out of my purse, and you didn't put it back, and now it doesn't even matter that we stopped. We still won't have pictures of Asheville for Mama Lacy."

"I don't know why you want pictures of that anyway. It's creepy."

Adam's backing away from us as our voices rise. "It's not creepy. She was a photographer! She loved pictures! She took pictures when we stopped at gas stations! She took pictures of sunrises and sunsets and all the moon phases! She took pictures of the first rain of spring and the first snow of winter and the first orange leaf of fall and she even took pictures of breakfast if it looked pretty! And she always, always, always took pictures on birthdays!"

"So?"

"So why wouldn't she want one final birthday picture?"

"Because it's creepy!" I say again, but really I'm thinking, *Because it's sad!* And then I process her meaning and a frown creases my forehead. "What do you mean, birthday picture?"

"You didn't even remember that her birthday's tomorrow—Today?" Zany sighs and shakes her head. "Why do you think we're doing this, anyway? I'm trying to give her a birthday present."

"I haven't been keeping track of the calendar," I murmur, but she's right. I ought to have remembered that it's Mama Lacy's birthday. "We haven't made a cake," I say, and then realize how stupid this sounds.

Zany doesn't answer. She's gone back to slamming

items into the cart. Once she starts holding a grudge, she'll never stop. Filling up the shopping cart is no longer fun for her. Adam, on the other hand, is really getting into this. By the time he tops off the cart with a fifty-pound bag of deer corn from the hunting section, he's laughing out loud. I trail along behind them, thinking of how we'd always made a cake on Mama Lacy's birthday—pie on Mama Shannon's and cookies on mine and cake for Mama Lacy and Zany—and how I can't believe I would have missed her birthday if Zany hadn't told me.

"What's the point of this?" Adam asks as his giggles finally fade. He seems to have noticed that Zany's no longer laughing, and he's heaving to push the overloaded buggy.

"That," Zany says, pointing to his face. The deep lines around his mouth are gone and he's got the ghost of a smile on his lips.

He smiles wider. Whispers barely loud enough for me to overhear, "I'm ready now."

She nods, keeping her sad gaze hidden behind a fake smile that doesn't reach her eyes. "Good." We leave the cart in the hunting aisle and return to the car without buying anything.

chapter
13

I see the brick hospital looming and my stomach feels knotted up. Zany's at the wheel and the truck jerks and swerves more than when Adam's driving, but that's not what's making me nervous. I don't know what we're going to do once we get there. Whether we're supposed to wait for Adam. Whether we'll be able to find another ride. It's after two in the morning and I'm absolutely not going to trust any more strangers on the road to take me where I'm going.

Unless, of course, Zany tells me to.

I don't have to know Adam well to recognize the look on his face. Mama Shannon wore that same look the whole last year of Mama Lacy's life. Our final coffee chat was three days before we lost Mama Lacy. She was at the hospital, which had happened before, but this time we knew she probably wasn't coming home. Mama Shannon was up even earlier than usual, slumped at the table, halfway through a pot of coffee before I found her in the kitchen. It was still dark outside.

"Can't sleep?" she asked, and when I shook my head, she said, "Me either. It's too quiet without Lace." The corners of her eyes pinched tight and she looked up at me. She wasn't wearing her glasses and I could see the redness, the folds of skin beneath her eyes turning into old-person wrinkles even though she wasn't that old. There weren't any tear tracks on her cheeks, but I remember thinking she was crying anyway, right there in front of me, in her own way.

"Mama," I said, and that was all I had to say. She opened her arms and I walked into them.

I've been dreaming scary things since Mama Lacy died. Sad things. Like how I found her hair in the shower drain. Like how Mama Shannon cried and cried at the memorial till Granny Culvert had to give her medicine to make her calm down.

If I was going to be stolen away by a grandmother, I wish it had been Granny Culvert, who'd chased her dreams, and a fella, off to Texas last time Mama Lacy was well. Granny Culvert, with her tangled braids and her rolled-up blue jeans, would have been comfortable to live with. But I was no blood relation to Granny Culvert and anyways she wouldn't have gotten custody. The stuffy judge responsible for deciding my future would never have handed me to a crazy old lady with purple hair who smoked Cuban cigars. No, it was Mrs. Madison, in her silk blouse with its high-button collar, who fussed at the judge until he agreed to take me away from Mama Shannon.

I don't want to be mad at Mama Shannon, but I am. She's my mother. Not legally—the law doesn't let two moms adopt each other's kids or get married or do any of the other things my mothers wanted to do—but she's still my mother. She should have been able to stop Mrs. Madison from taking me away. She'd been so upset over Mama Lacy, so sad and tired and unable to get out of bed in the mornings, that even the judge could see how my clothes were dirty in court and how Mama Shannon had no energy and barely any voice.

Oh, she asked for me. Begged the judge not to take me. But her fingers kept picking at each other till they bled, and under the fluorescent lights of the courthouse, you could really see the saggy tear bags under her eyes. If I were the judge, I might not have let her keep me, either.

Still, I can't help thinking if I'd done better in court, if I'd remembered to wash my face and if I'd hung up my clothes so the wrinkles fell out, maybe the judge would have given me to Mama Shannon for keeps. But he didn't and now I'm not hers anymore.

Zany tosses her cigarette out my window. I watch it whip by in the wind and scatter sparks on the pavement behind us in the dark. My eyes are feeling heavy, and everything is slow, like the scary part in a movie, inching by, with dark music playing. Only the thing that's playing now is the country station and Adam's soft voice is singing along.

He turns off the radio as Zany hits the emergency flashers and parks in the fire lane.

"Think they'll let you in?" she asks.

He doesn't look at her. "They told me they would." From the way his voice sounds, I don't think that's a good thing. They don't usually let people visit other people in the hospital at this hour. Not unless there's a reason to hurry.

"Hop out," Zany says. Her voice is low. "I'll park the truck."

"Thanks." He doesn't sound like he's even paying attention. I think about how all the things that happened as Mama Lacy passed blur together when I try

118

to remember them, and I wonder what Adam will remember about us, whether he'll ever think about two girls who ought to have had a laugh track policing his car-burglaring, or whether we'll be lost in the haze of the worst night he's had to face.

He walks away without looking back, and Zany watches the door until he's been out of sight for almost a minute.

Then she pulls the truck around the emergency loop and drives toward the parking garage.

Past the parking garage.

Toward the EXIT sign and the road beyond.

"Zany!"

"Shh."

"Zany! What are you—"

"Be quiet."

"But you're—"

"Oh my god." She pulls over to the shoulder and whips around to look at me, foot jammed on the brake. "I know. Okay? You don't have to freak out and tell me I'm stealing a car, because I know I'm stealing a car, and I know all the reasons it's a bad idea, and I know I'm going to go to jail. Okay? Wow. Just stop talking. Stop. Talking."

"It's not a car. It's a truck." In case they put you in

jail longer for a truck than they would for a car. I don't know. Don't figure Zany does, either. She's got her eyes closed and she's blowing out a long breath through her lips. When she opens her eyes, her whole face has turned pink.

"Stop. Talking."

"But we just stopped Adam from stealing money. Now we're going to steal a whole truck?"

"We're not stealing the truck. We're borrowing the truck."

"But you just said—"

"Oh my *god*! Ophelia. You have to stop talking, or so help me, I will leave you here. I will put you out by the side of the road and I will drive away."

"You wouldn't really."

"You want to find out? Jesus." She throws in a couple of swearwords as she lifts her foot off the brake and eases us back into traffic.

There's a world of room in the front seat of the truck without Adam, and I turn my back against the door and pull my feet up on the seat. I'm facing Zany in case she decides to talk to me, but I won't start talking to her first. She's so worked up, I can see her mouth moving in the semidarkness, whispering to herself. I wonder whether she's planning the route or rehearsing what to say to Mama Shannon when she finds out about all this.

I lay my head back against the window and try to nap, but now that we've scooted farther apart and I'm not squished up against Zany, I'm cold. I don't dare mention it, because Zany doesn't have any sleeves on at all, thanks to me, and at least I've got my robe. I've also got Haberdashery snuggled up warm against my thigh.

The billboards next to the interstate catch my eye. They advertise fun things like amusement parks and petting zoos, historical monuments and shopping centers. I remember stopping along the way with our mothers, back when we were traveling the other direction. I remember Mama Lacy buying me a stuffed pony I've still got, only it's back at Mrs. Madison's.

"Something pretty for my pretty," she'd said. I only felt pretty when Mama Lacy said it.

I remember petting a llama with Mama Shannon, and letting a Ferris wheel swoop me and Zany up into the clouds. Mama Lacy made me feel pretty, but Mama Shannon made me feel like an adventurer.

We don't stop at any of the billboard places now. The brass container in my hand is feeling heavier with every mile. I close my eyes and let the signs pass without looking at them.

chapter
14

It's easy to dream about driving back from Asheville. I was sleepy then, too, passing miles in a car with a heater that couldn't keep up. It was December, almost Christmas, and we'd been looking forward to New Year's fireworks over the courthouse. We'd been looking forward to a lot of things we were never going to have.

It started well before that, back when I was six. Mama Lacy came home from the doctor, and for a week or two, all our mothers could do was whisper-worry, and whisper-fight, and whisper-worry some more. These were the parents who had laughed us through the chicken pox and fevers and the flu. I had never heard them whisper-worry or whisper-fight before.

Doctor visits came and went, little appointment cards stuck to the refrigerator with magnets I made in art class. Worry tipped over into silliness. We would go out and get chocolate cake for breakfast, or stay home from school to roller-skate, or watch movies till three a.m. on weeknights. Mama Lacy stopped going to work. She couldn't dance with us anymore, so we put her in charge of the music. She started wearing scarves that matched not just her outfits but the rooms she and Mama Shannon had painted in the brightest of their favorite colors. She always, always smiled when she caught me looking at her, but I wasn't always able to smile back.

Mac and cheese turned into butter noodles. Real milk to powdered. Cinnamon Toast Crunch to cornflakes. Then the boxes showed up. Some marked EGGS. Some marked CHARMIN. They came by the trunk load from the grocery store, empty, and got packed in the car a week later, full. Not full of eggs and toilet paper, but of our lives, loosely sorted by room. *Kitchen Stuff. Bedroom Stuff. Give Away. Keep.*

I was seven. I knew we were moving back to West Virginia, but mostly I was excited about the road trip and our late dinner at Mack and Morello's. It wasn't until we were sitting in the restaurant that it hit me:

We would not be coming back to Asheville.

We would not be coming back to Mack and Morello's with its orange floor and its familiar, twinkling lights.

We would not be coming back to our apartment, which we left all alone.

Now that it was time to go, I finally thought of my yellow bedroom. My toes curled up, missing the blue linoleum in the kitchen. My fingers opened, as if reaching for the glass doorknob to the closet. I hadn't said goodbye to the building. I had only packed the little things, not the painted walls and the carpet and the comforting surfaces of the only home I knew. I thought about my handwriting on the boxes. *Give Away. Keep.* In the end it wasn't up to me. It didn't matter what I wrote.

When my hand came open, the plate slipped out. It was a flimsy paper plate, nothing breakable, but the way the ketchup and mustard splattered, I couldn't stop looking. Orange floor. Red ketchup. Yellow mustard. Orange floor I'd never walk on again. Red ketchup, yellow mustard that would never taste right after that. The radio played, quiet. Something happy. Nobody ate, but we sat there long enough we could have eaten twice. Afterward, we drove and drove, exactly like this.

I remember waking up now and then. I can still remember the crinkles in Zany's forehead and the way, just for a while, just on that trip, it seemed natural to call her Zoey Grace. It's strange she was about the age then that I am now.

Back in West Virginia, things were different. Mama Lacy got sicker and me and Zany couldn't ever manage to say the right thing. And Mama Shannon, Mama Shannon was a basket case. She went back and forth between stern and distracted, putting her car keys in the refrigerator and the hot dogs on the coffee table, then getting mad at us for leaving the hot dogs out or for losing her car keys.

After a while, though, things got better. Mama Lacy got better.

My dreams don't let me stay in that part.

I skip ahead years, to when the cancer returned. Appointment cards on the refrigerator, this time the magnets store-bought. This time nobody talking about anything. Everybody was calm.

That night last year, in the hospital corridor, I rocked from toe to heel, heel to toe. I tugged at my skirt and itched in my sweater. I kicked at my pointy-toed shoes. Mrs. Madison had come over to get me ready to go, and she picked my clothes. I longed for jeans and sneakers. I couldn't bear to stay still and quiet in the waiting room, yet all there was to do was wait.

Mrs. Madison had to give Mama Shannon permission

to go in to see Mama Lacy. Mrs. Madison, who Mama Lacy could just barely be civil with, was allowed to go in, and Mama Shannon, who had spent the last sixteen years at Mama Lacy's side, had to ask permission. In North Carolina, it was OK. In North Carolina, they had done all the paperwork years ago to make decisions for each other, but now we'd moved home, and with Mama Lacy sick, we couldn't afford to do all the right papers again. Watching one mama ask permission to see the other, it felt like all the air left the building for a minute. Even once I started breathing again, I felt like something had changed for good.

Something about Mama Shannon's face when she asked Mrs. Madison to let her in to the ICU was going to stick with me. Every time I sleep, I go back to those moments, cold linoleum and a scratchy sweater. I can smell the disinfectant and hear the clock ticking. Sometimes I think I won't ever wake up.

chapter
15

The heater's off and everything feels shifted, like time has passed. It's so dark I can't see where I am and for a minute I think I'm still asleep and dreaming. But I never know I'm dreaming in my dreams, so that can't be true.

I sit up and the seat belt pulls against my shoulder, which is the first reminder I'm in a truck. I can't see anything through the windshield except a set of headlights going the other way, and in their light, snow has started to fall. The car passes us and the windows fade to dark.

I feel like I've been asleep for a hundred hours, but the sky's not light yet. Beside me, Zany is dozing with her forehead on the steering wheel. It takes me a really long time to puzzle out that we're parked on the shoulder of the highway in the middle of the night. Even longer to figure out why.

I'm about to wake Zany and then I remember she's the driver, and maybe she ought to sleep a little more if she's going to continue to be the driver. I'm too tired to argue with her anyway and that's what we do when we're both awake.

A phone rings.

We don't have a phone, so this strikes me as odd. I remember that Adam had one and wonder where it ended up. Still groggy with sleep, I feel around in the darkness and my hand discovers the ringing cell phone wedged under the front seat.

I hit the green button to answer half a second before I realize that this is Adam's phone, and answering it means I'm in his truck, which is proof I helped *steal* his truck. I stab buttons, trying to end the call before the police I'm certain are on the other end can get a trace.

But then I hear a voice say, "Hello?" all distant and tinny, and it doesn't sound like the police. Cringing, I lift the phone to my ear and wait for the voice to come again.

"I know you're there, Zany," Adam says after a minute.

"Oh. Hi." Relief and sleep work together and my voice comes out low and rough.

"Zany?"

"Uh-uh, she's sleeping. This is Fella."

"Oh." A pause. "So you *did* steal my truck."

"No, um . . . I mean, no, this is Fella. Zany stole your truck."

"Of course she did." He laughs once, short. "I knew I liked her. I'd have done the same damn thing. Is it still in one piece, the truck?"

I fiddle with the broken air vent at my knees. "I mean, as much as it was before."

He snorts a breath that might be a laugh. Then says, "It's my dad's truck. He's never let anybody else drive it before. I couldn't believe it when he told me he'd left it for me and he wanted me to bring it. He's so worried about the truck. With everything else to worry about, he wants to know where the truck is and if I'm being careful with it."

I remember a parking lot in the early morning when Zany turned fifteen, Mama Shannon in the passenger seat of the Subaru and my sister behind the wheel. I remember starts and stops, starts and stops, while I sat on the sidewalk nearby, scratching stick figures with a rock on the concrete.

"Mom didn't want me to drive it," Adam says. "She didn't want me to come. She doesn't get along with him. They haven't talked in years. Even . . ." He sighs and swears. "Even *now*."

I don't really know what to say. I know a little something about families not getting along. Even before Mama Lacy died, back when she was just sick, we had our share of fighting in my family. Mama Lacy tried over and over again to get Mrs. Madison to be as nice to Mama Shannon and Zany as she was to me. Not that Mrs. Madison was unkind—she was perfectly polite, always invited my family in, offered them coffee and pop and deviled eggs or whatever she had in the fridge—but that was part of the problem. She treated Mama Shannon and Zoey Grace as guests in her home. Guests, not family.

I can't think what to say to help Adam, but the silence has gone on long enough, so I say, "We're not stealing your car!" My voice gets higher-pitched, and Zany stirs in her sleep. Forcing myself to speak more quietly, I repeat, "We're not. We're only borrowing it. We'll get it back to you in the morning."

"It's morning already," Adam says. "Practically four. How far'd you guys get?"

I hesitate, wondering if he has the police on the line. Then I realize it doesn't matter. I have no idea where we are.

"I don't know. I've been sleeping. Now it's Zany's turn to sleep."

There's a silence.

"I'm sorry about your truck," I add. "We really will bring it right back. I know it was crazy to take it. I know, it's just, you weren't using it for the next little while, and Zany has this thing about how we *have* to scatter Mama Lacy *today* because it's her birthday. Can you picture that, your birthday only coming every four years? She liked to joke about how much younger she was than Mama Shannon."

"So you all, like, have a spare mom, then."

I immediately tense up. People aren't always nice about the two-moms thing.

"Not anymore," I say pointedly, and I hear the air punch out of him.

"Right," he says. "Sorry."

"Well . . . look, are you going to call the police?" I ask, just as Adam says, "I can't face him."

I'm too flustered, and it's too dark, and I can't keep up. "Can't face who? What?"

"You're just a kid. You can't—I can't—my dad."

More of the cobwebs clear. I sit up straighter. "You can't face your dad?"

His sigh rattles over the line. "I've been standing in the hallway for over an hour."

My brain slams into panic mode when it sinks in

131

that this means we dropped Adam off over an hour ago. Have we been sleeping ever since? I wonder how far Zany drove before she pulled us over. How completely late we are on our mission.

He should go in, I think. But I can't tell him that. We're in his truck, talking on his phone. He's doing us a favor, not calling the police. So I wait.

"He probably won't even stick around till morning. Which—isn't even—I can't—I don't even want to think about that right now. I can't go in."

"Adam—"

But now that he's told me his problem, he's quick to dodge. "Hey—y'all are famous. I saw you on TV."

This makes me sit up straighter still. Even though he's only trying to change the subject, I have to find out what he means. "We're on TV?" I open my arms and let Haberdashery crawl up into my lap. He turns in a circle and settles down to sleep.

"The news put your pictures up in case anybody's seen you. They don't know which direction you're headed or nothing, but you should call your mom. She's worried."

"My mom? Not just Mrs. Madison?" I'm thinking of the earlier radio broadcast.

"No, she said she was your mom, and she mentioned

both of you. They've got a news alert out and every-body's looking for you. The police called your mom about her car being abandoned, I guess, because they say you might be hitchhiking or that somebody might have you."

Guilt rushes through me. I think of Mama Shannon as I last saw her, asleep on the sofa in her tiny apartment. Think of her waking to find Zany gone, checking the driveway and not seeing the car, checking her voice messages. Being worried enough to check with Mrs. Madison and discover I was gone, too. Or maybe it had happened the other way around. Maybe she was awakened by a ringing phone and it was Mrs. Madison calling to find out whether she'd taken me back in the middle of the night. My brain starts cooking up a scenario in which Mrs. Madison sent the police to Mama Shannon's house, and that's how she got woken up—by a big, booming knock on her door. All because of me and Zany—as if she didn't look tired and sad enough already.

"Are you going to call her?" Adam asks. "I mean, you've got my phone. Why not call her?"

"Hey, how *are* you calling me, when I've got your phone?" Two can play the changing-subject game.

"Well, since I don't own the only phone ever invented in the world, I'm using a pay phone."

"You should go in."

He swallows so loud I can hear it through the phone. "I can't talk to my dad. I can't talk to him when he's well. I can't talk to him ever. What am I supposed to say now that's not going to come out wrong?"

"Everything's going to come out wrong. You do it anyway." I sniffle, partly from the cold and partly from something else.

"Did what you said come out wrong?" he asks in a voice almost pleading.

I fiddle with the crooked heat vent till the cover comes off in my hand. I hope Adam can't hear me breaking his truck. I catch my breath and get ready to confess.

"I didn't say nothing," I admit. "I stood in the hallway till it was too late."

There's a long, cold silence and then Adam says, "I'm going in, okay? I'm going to try." And, quieter, "You should try, too."

chapter

16

"Mama Shannon?"

"Oh my god. Where are you, Fella? Are you okay?"
Mama Shannon can't fit enough words into the fast
talking she's trying to do, but I get the idea. I know she's
frantic, but it's almost a comfort to hear something other
than tired sadness in her voice.

"We're okay. We just—we had somewhere to be. Just
for a little bit. We won't be too long."

"Fella, where *are* you?"

"I don't know. Zany's in charge and she's asleep. I
just didn't want you to worry. You—I heard you were
worried."

"Of course I'm worried! I wake up to find out my

girls are gone in the night from both their beds? What am I supposed to think happened?"

"You're supposed to think we're together and, as long as we're together, we're okay."

She breathes in and out and in again so quickly that I think she might be about to cry. "Honey, I need to come get you."

"You can't. We broke your car."

"I'll get there. I'll leave right now. You just tell me where I'm going."

"Mama, we'll be—we'll be home in the morning, okay? I love you." I sniffle, gasp in hard to keep from crying out loud. "I'm sorry we scared you. I love you, okay? I'll see you soon."

I end the call to find Zany staring at me, awake, from the driver's seat.

"Who was that?"

"Nobody."

"Where did you get that? Is that Adam's phone? He didn't take it with him?"

"It was under the seat. I guess it came out of his pocket, or he was so frazzled he forgot it. I can't believe you slept through it ringing and me talking. You must have been tired."

"Talking to who?"

136

"Adam called. He noticed the truck was gone."

She pushes herself up a little straighter in her seat. "Did he call the cops?"

"Nah. He's busy. I told him we'd get it back by morning. And he saw us on TV."

This catches her attention. "Both of us?"

"Mama Shannon was worried."

"Mad worried or scared worried?"

"Both, and cry-worried, too."

Zany swears. "I didn't want to scare her."

"But what did you think was going to happen?"

The phone in my hand starts ringing then, making me jump a mile. I quickly hit the red button to hang up on the caller before Zany can find out it's Mama Shannon.

She had just been about to turn the key in the ignition, and now she's stopped again. "Who was that?"

"Nobody."

"Fella—"

"Do you have to go to the bathroom yet? Because I have to go to the bathroom."

"Fella."

The phone starts to ring again, and again, I hit the End button. Then the Power button to turn the thing off entirely. "Maybe we should let you sleep a little longer," I suggest, watching her fight a yawn.

"No, if I go to sleep again, who knows who you'll call? And we'd better not sit still too long if our faces are out there." She was not thrilled to hear about Adam seeing us on the news.

"Well then, let's at least stop for pie or something. I'm starving." I point to a Waffle House logo on a big blue sign that announces attractions for the upcoming exit.

"Ophelia. We cannot stop at a Waffle House when there's an alert out for us."

"Oh, yeah." Now all I want is pie. My stomach growls and I know Zany hears it, because she sighs.

"All right. Here's the deal. You're going to stay in the truck. I'm going to go in and get us something to eat and bring it out to you. If there's only one of us, we won't look nearly as suspicious." She pulls the truck onto the road.

"And you'll get pie?"

"Geez. Yes, okay? I heard you. Pie."

"And you'll bring something for Haberdashery?" He wags his little nub tail when he hears his name.

"I'll get him something, just not pie," Zany offers.

We get off at the exit, but Zany is so tired she drives right past the Waffle House. It's still snowing, not enough to make the roads slick, but enough to make the inside of the truck seem sleepy and cozy. I have to nudge Zany and point, and she drives two more blocks before she finds a good place to turn around.

"Oak Street," she says, gazing at the neat row of houses next to the green street sign. "I wonder what it's like to live on Oak Street in . . . in wherever-we-are, Virginia." She sounds homesick, but I don't get why. The houses here are small and sweet, and I think again of the crummy apartment she and Mama Shannon share. I want Mama Shannon and Zany to have a better place to live. Someplace like where I'm living, bright and safe.

At the Waffle House, Zany parks several spaces from the door. As the truck motor dies, I have second thoughts.

"Maybe they've seen you on TV. Maybe they'll turn you in. Maybe we—"

"Shouldn't do this," Zany finishes for me. "You've got to stop saying that, kid." She shrugs. "Maybe they've seen us, okay? Maybe they have. And then we get caught and we get sent back and we have to try again, but, Fella, I'm *tired* of *shouldn't*. There were so many things in Mama Lacy's life she wanted to do that she didn't do because she *shouldn't*."

"Like what?"

"Like doing things alone. Do you remember how

much she wanted to hike the Appalachian Trail all by herself?"

"I don't know, maybe."

"Well, she did. She wanted to get out in the woods alone and figure things out? But she didn't, because you don't do that if you've got kids and a wife and a job. She put it off and put it off and now she'll never get to do it. Or what about her singing? She loved to sing all those old songs, but she got so embarrassed if anybody heard. Why shouldn't she have gotten to sing in front of everybody? Why can't people just do the stuff they want to do before it's too late?"

"And you think scattering her is going to fix it?" I huff out a mad breath. "I still need her, Zany."

Zany's got the longest sigh anywhere. When she stops sighing, she reaches over to rub the urn like it'll help her think. "Fella, I thought you were with me on this. We've got to do what she wanted."

Before she's finished talking, I shove the truck door open, hard, and climb out. "Come on, then. I'm going with you. We'll just hope they don't recognize us, since we have to do everything your way."

"But your dog—"

She hasn't even finished the sentence before I've turned around to secure him. I make sure the windows are rolled up with a little gap for air, and that the doors are locked so he can't get out. We're not doing *that* again! I don't want to leave him in the truck. Mama Lacy once threatened to call the police and Mama Shannon almost broke a window to rescue a dog left in a hot car. But it's the middle of the night and cold, so I think he'll be okay.

Zany follows me across the parking lot with another long sigh. "They've been at work all night, Fella. How do you figure they've been watching TV? There's no way they'll recognize us."

I push through the door without answering. The bright yellow diner is open twenty-four hours, but at this hour, it's deserted except for the cooks and waitresses, who are singing along with the radio. Everybody's wearing stripes and the lights and patterns and color are too much for my sleepy eyes. I squint and fall back a step, letting Zany catch up.

"Good morning, y'all," an energetic waitress bellows. I'm startled by the word *morning*. I think it ought to still be night.

"Good morning," Zany says wearily, dragging herself into the nearest booth. I slide in across from her and start studying the shiny menu, using it to hide the bright ketchup and mustard bottles from my view.

"Out early today, are we?" the waitress notices,

snatching up a pen and a pad of striped paper. "What can I get you ladies to drink?"

"A Pepsi," I say. "Or a Coke, whatever you got."

Zany rubs her eyes. "Can I get a coffee and a Mountain Dew?" She dumps a pile of quarters on the counter.

"We don't serve Mountain Dew. You want I should bring you a Sprite?"

"There's no caffeine in Sprite!" Zany sounds shocked. "I'd like coffee, please. Lots of it. Black."

"How old are you?"

"Why?" I can tell Zany's trying to make her face look older by the pinched look on it. "Is there an age limit for coffee?"

"Kid, I'm just asking." The waitress holds up her hand.

"Do you have pecan pie?" I ask.

"Good thinking! Sugar is good!" Zany chimes in.

The waitress gives her an odd look but delivers the pie and our drinks. Zany heaps four spoonfuls of sugar into her coffee, then gives up on the spoon and dumps sugar in straight from the jar.

"Zany, can I have a dollar?" I ask. I've spotted the jukebox. Zany's taken charge of my sock money like she has just about everything else on this trip, from taking Mama Lacy in the first place to stealing the truck.

She hands over the dollar without a word, and I jump up and start scanning the songs. Some of the titles are familiar from a hundred years ago. I think maybe we listened to these same songs on the way to West Virginia from Asheville with Mama Shannon and Mama Lacy.

"Remember this?" I ask Zany, and I start one of the songs we used to listen to, Sister Hazel's "Just Remember." I'm proud to remember something that maybe Zany doesn't, but of course she does. A smile plays across her lips and I look at her dry, dry eyes. I wonder if she ever cries. Zany takes the longest drink of hot coffee I've ever seen anyone take without stopping to breathe. Then she leaps from the booth to grab my hand and we spin around the diner between the syrup-sticky booths, feet slipping on the checkered floor.

Our waitress is smiling with her whole face, mouth, eyes—something nobody in my family has done in a long time. When she sees me looking, she glances away, but I get shy anyway and slide back into the booth.

"We used to dance to this with Mama Lacy, didn't we?" Zany asks, breathless, falling back into her seat. "While Mama Shannon was at work."

"Yep," I say, pleased that I remember.

"And you would dress up in Mama Lacy's work

clothes and you thought you looked so cool with her chicken shirt and her paper hat."

That part I don't remember. Maybe. The shirt had red stripes? I sigh. I must have been pretty little at the time. It was probably one of the jobs Mama Lacy cycled through to support our family and her passion for photography.

"It's not fair, you know," I say.

"What's not fair?"

"That you're always going to be older than me."

She laughs. "Not much you can do about that."

"But you remember the best stuff and I've forgotten almost all of it." I stab my pie with my fork so hard a pecan splits in two.

"What don't you remember?" Zany asks.

"Well, I can't know unless I remember, can I?" I point out, frustrated.

"All right, then. What *do* you remember?"

"About Mama Lacy?"

"Yeah. And the time we lived in Asheville."

"I remember dancing. All the time, dancing. Mama Lacy had so much energy back then. And I remember eating a lot of chicken for dinner."

"That's because Mama Lacy had that chicken job."

"And Mama Shannon worked at a different phone company back then."

"Yeah, she had the tool belt and she had to climb the poles."

I nod. "I do remember that. She let me try on her spiky boots one time and climb up as high as her head."

"Me, too."

I stop stabbing the pie and start eating, big bites, till my plate is empty except for the little square I'm saving for Haberdashery. Zany's barely started on hers, but I notice she's drunk half the coffee already.

When the bell above the door jingles, I glance up and freeze.

"Zany." I try to talk without moving my lips, which is apparently the going method for talking when there are police around. I nod slightly toward the police officer, certain he's come in to arrest us.

"Relax," she whispers back, and takes another bite of her pie. She's acting natural, but I can tell she's watching the cop out of the corner of her eye. I'm glad our song's over. I would hate for "Just Remember" to always remind me of the day I got arrested.

The officer sits down in the booth next to ours, with a tremendous jingle as all his keys and handcuffs and possibly weapons settle themselves into the booth along with him. I drop my face onto my arms. I was hoping he'd go sit at the far end.

Still, I'm curious what cops eat. He orders a BLT with no mayo and enjoys a cup of coffee. I say enjoys because I can hear him sipping and sighing and making tiny, happy noises into the cup. His radio crackles and bleats, but never makes a noise I recognize, although he nods like he understands the sounds it makes.

Zany wolfs down the rest of her pie and chugs her coffee so fast I know it's all going to hit her brain at once and we're going to be lucky if she doesn't take off and fly through the ceiling. She's hustling me out of the booth by the elbow when the cop says, without looking at us, "Up early, aren't you?"

Zany stops so fast I step on her heel.

"Us?" she asks in a squeak too small to have come from my brave sister. I start feeling uncertain, dancing from foot to foot. I'm not used to Zany being unsure.

Now the cop looks up. His face isn't unfriendly, but I scoot closer to my sister anyways and she loops an arm through mine to steady me.

"I have a girl close to your age," he says to Zany. "I don't think I'd let her roam about at this hour in the cold. Not even five in the morning yet. Just wonderin'."

Zany looks at me and blushes. "I wanted to treat my baby sister to some pie. She got an A on her big math test." Which I'm certain he can tell is a lie simply by looking at me, because, clearly, I am not the A-making type, and certainly not in math. A students in math can at least match the right number of socks to shoes. I wrap my left ankle around my right one to hide the purple sock peeking out.

"So you take her out at five in the morning? Your parents let you do that?"

Zany blushes again and looks at the floor. I start to get the feeling she's holding my arm to steady herself, not me. "Not exactly," she admits. "We . . . kind of didn't tell them."

The cop nods. Seems to appreciate Zany's honesty, because he doesn't know it's not completely honest honesty. I'm preoccupied by my panicking. Five? It's already five in the morning?

"I see." He studies us. "Do you live far?"

"A couple blocks up the road. On Oak Street."

The officer nods slowly, then flashes us a smile. "I'm gonna drive up that way in twenty minutes and I'd better not see you still roaming," he says. "And make sure you tell your parents before you head out at this hour again."

We nod furiously. Zany tugs me toward the door and I'm careful to keep my free arm crossed over my robe so he can't see Haberdashery's blood. He might think I've murdered somebody and that's why we're sneaking around. We make it out into the swirling flurries, where Zany starts laughing frantically. Her laugh doesn't sound like anything is funny. I wish she hadn't had so much coffee.

In the car, Zany sits for a minute behind the wheel, gathering courage. She's careful to pull out in the direction of Oak Street, traveling almost three blocks before she loops around toward the interstate.

chapter
17

By the time the interstate takes us
from Virginia into Tennessee at half past five, we're singing along to a radio song we barely know. Zany's making
up words and Haberdashery's yipping and howling at all
the right spots. I'm humming the guitar riffs and tapping
out the rhythm on the dashboard.

"See, this isn't so bad," Zany says between songs.
"This is what a road trip's supposed to be like. Fun and
singing. You're having a good time, aren't you?"

I'm reluctant to admit it, but she's right. "Yeah, I
guess." The sugar revived me. My glum mood from earlier is gone and I'm enjoying the music.

I'm even sort of enjoying Zany, just a little bit. It's nice
to be alone with her, just the two of us, like grown-ups.

"*A*," she says out of the blue when the music gives way to commercials. "*Texaco* has an *A* in it."

"Huh?" I see the Texaco station but have no idea why she's pointing it out.

"The alphabet game!"

"Oh." I start scanning the signs, but Zany spots a *B* first.

"*Biltmore*!" She points to a billboard. "See, there are already ads for stuff in Asheville. We're not that far away!"

Dread swims in my stomach. "Please don't do this," I say.

"Do what? Beat you at the alphabet game?"

I touch the urn. I don't want Zany to get mad at me, but this is important. We're getting close enough to Asheville that there are billboards for its attractions by the highway. I've got to get her convinced before we arrive.

"Don't scatter her. Just because you want to doesn't mean we all do."

Zany grips the steering wheel harder. "We're on *C*," she says. "You better keep looking."

"Time-out. Zany—"

"Doesn't matter what any of us want except her."

I do remember when Mama Lacy wanted to hike the Appalachian Trail. I hadn't thought about it in years

150

until Zany brought it up, but when she reminds me that Mama Lacy's wishes are what matter now, I think of it again. I was little, maybe six. I didn't want her to go away from me. I begged and begged her not to go.

It worked, that time. And at six years old, I was happy, but at twelve, I'm thinking about what Zany said before, that Mama Lacy will never get the chance to hike the trail now. And she'll never sing in public and she'll never run outside in the first spring rain the way she always loved to do. Every single thing Mama Lacy has ever done is in the past, and there won't be anything else.

What Mama Lacy wanted matters. It does. But I still don't know how to stop wishing that I didn't have to let her go. "Zany—"

"Time-in. Start looking for the next letter."

I bounce on the seat in frustration. Zany won't listen to me at all. But she's peering into the darkness and I know she's going to find a C first. Suddenly I can't stand to have her beat me at this stupid game. I squint at the next road sign as our headlights flash across it, lighting up grime from coal trucks and streaks of muddy snow melt and, underneath, the letter C.

Zany gets there first. "C!" she says. "*Comfort Inn*!"

"Dang!" I hate when Zany finds all the letters before me. I start looking for *E* instead of *D*, figuring she'll surely find *D* before me and then I'll be ready with an *E*, but then an *Exxon* sign flies by and I can't even say it because Zany hasn't found *D* yet.

Just when I find a *McDonald's* sign, Zany shouts, "*D*! *Days Inn*!"

"Stop it! Give me a chance!"

And then she says, "*E*! *Speed limit*!" I smack her on the arm and sniffle back my tears. They aren't about the game. They've just been waiting at the surface for something to poke a hole so they could get out. But Zany doesn't notice. She's still rubbing her stinging arm. "Quit it, brat! I can't help it if you suck at the alphabet!"

"*G*!" I shout, pointing at a *Golden Corral* sign. I am *going* to win this game.

"We're on *F*," Zany corrects me. "Speaking of which, *Food City*."

"*G*!" I screech, pointing in the rearview mirror. "*Golden Corral*! You can still see it!"

"No, the sign has to be in front of you or it doesn't count," Zany says.

"You just made up that rule!"

"Did not! That's always been the rule!"

"No, it hasn't!" I slam against the door and cross my arms over my chest. "I'm not playing with you! You're a cheater and I don't play with cheaters!"

"Fine," Zany says. "If it makes you feel better to tell yourself that, that's fine."

Half a second later, I sit up straighter. "Ooh! G! *Garden Center*!" I point to a Super Wal-Mart.

"I thought you weren't playing," Zany says. "*H. Home Depot*."

"*I*!" My voice is just this side of loud enough to shatter glass. "*Speed Limit* again!"

"You can't reuse—"

"Oh, you can *too* reuse signs! Stop making up rules!"

"Fine!" she screeches. She's sunk to my level. "*J*! *Flying J Truck Stop*!"

"The letter can't be all by itself," I say. "It has to be part of a word."

"Does not! Now you're making up rules!"

"Well, if you get to make up rules, I get to make up rules!"

"So you admit you made it up!" Zany hollers. "That means it doesn't count! Next is *K*! The *K* in *Flying J Truck Stop* counts! Then *L*! *Left Lane Closed*! I got two!" She laughs triumphantly before her face gets serious. "Wait, left lane closed? For real?"

We swish around a turn and Zany hits the brakes to get us slowed down. Ten or fifteen cars have bottlenecked trying to get into the open lane.

153

"*M*," I say. "*Man*, it sucks to run into another traffic jam."

"*N*." Zany giggles. "*Nobody* here knows how to drive, or we wouldn't be stuck waiting for people to scoot into the right lane!"

"*O*! *Oh*, gosh, can these people not drive!"

"*P*! *Please* get in the right lane, people!" We both dissolve into giggles.

The car in front of us squeezes through the traffic jam, and we follow. Soon we're back up to seventy. After a while, I notice a shopping plaza sign with all kinds of good words.

"What letter are we on?" I ask Zany.

"I don't know. Let's start over. And let's say it has to be the first letter of a word. It'll make it last longer."

"Okay," I say. "*A*. *Asheville*." I give up on real signs and say the sign I'm dreading. It won't be long before it looms in front of us.

"*A*," Zany repeats, "is definitely for *Asheville*." Her voice is hopeful, like she can't wait to see that stupid sign by the road.

Neither one of us bothers pointing out the letter *B* anywhere. We're stuck on *Asheville*, drawing closer and closer.

chapter
18

I remember coming down the mountain years ago, but driving up it in the February snow is entirely different. I see Zany's knuckles turning white from her grip on the wheel, and she spins the dial to silence the radio.

"What are you doing?"

"Playing pinochle."

"What's pinochle?"

"How should I know? What do you mean, what am I doing, Light Bulb? I'm driving."

Sisters. Geez. "I know that, Zany, I see that you're driving. I meant why did you turn down the radio?"

"Then why didn't you ask why I turned down the

radio? That's not what you asked. You asked, What am I doing."

Sometimes I don't understand how Zany and I end up in a fight. All it takes is for me to say one little thing that sounded perfectly simple to my own ears, and she gets mad at me for no reason. "Forget it!"

She drives on a little ways, then says, "It was distracting me. It keeps getting fuzzy."

"Is it the weather?"

"It's the mountains. *And* the weather. It's making me nervous."

The flurries have picked up into actual snow, hitting the windshield with a wet hiss. I don't want Zany to be distracted, because the road gets scarier the higher we go. There are drop-offs on the other side of the guard rail. But I do miss the radio. The voice in the background was something to hold on to.

"Zany?"

"Yeah."

"Will it distract you if I tell you something?"

I wait to see if she's going to get mad, but she only shakes her head a little. "Tell me."

"I did something bad." I'm thinking about Mama Lacy's letter and how I stole it.

"What did you do?"

156

"Well, I'm not going to tell you. But it was bad."

"Fella. You can't just say you did something bad and then not tell me what. Was it something dangerous?"

"No!" Now I wonder if she's picturing something *really* bad, like drinking or shoplifting or something. "No. It's not dangerous, it's just . . . kinda mean?"

"You? Mean? Never!"

"Hey, I'm not mean!"

"I just said that."

"But you were teasing, right?"

"I don't know, was I?" Bigger flakes start spinning down from the clouds, wet and thick. The truck weaves a little as Zany gets a handle on the weather, and Haberdashery hops into my lap and smushes his head under my chin. I hold him tighter. He's not the only one starting to worry about the roads.

"It's only a snowstorm, you two, relax!" Zany says, not sounding at all relaxed. She slows to fifty and hunches over the steering wheel, looking awfully nervous for only a snowstorm. Snow coats the glass and the windshield isn't see-through for a minute as Zany struggles to turn on the lazy windshield wipers.

"Shoot!" she hollers. The left wiper—the one in front of her—spins away into the gray morning. It must have already been broken most of the way off.

I guess that's the best we could expect from Adam's truck.

"Stupid Adam," I groan, "not fixing his windshield wiper."

Zany ignores me, or maybe she can't hear me. She swerves into the slow lane.

"Be careful!" I warn her. "It might be slippery!"

"Because you're an expert!" She slams the brakes and the truck fishtails.

I shriek. "Stop it!" Scared as I am, it doesn't take much to get me mad.

"Kind of busy!" She's still trying to get the truck moving straight.

"Well, you're not doing a very good job!"

"Oh, lighten up."

And I really hate when Zany tells me to lighten up. I smack her arm before I can stop myself. Not hard. Just hard enough to feel a little better.

"Quit it!" Now she sounds irritated, jerking her arm out of range. She turns to face me. "No hitting! Especially not when I'm driving in the—whoa!" She spins to face the road again as we slide on the slick pavement. She manages to get the truck stopped on the shoulder of the road as I snatch Haberdashery up to my chest. I can feel our hearts pounding.

"Says who?" I demand once the truck is under control. I look around. "Nobody here but you and me and Haberdashery and I don't think he cares if I hit you!"

"Says Mama Lacy!" Zany shoots back. "Wasn't she always telling you that she knew you could control yourself better? Of course I think that might be the only thing she was ever wrong about."

I can't help it. I slap Zany again, harder this time. Hard enough it leaves a red spot. I'm immediately ashamed and flustered. Zany just rescued us from a crash, and here I am hitting her. I know Mama Lacy would be disappointed if she could see me.

"Mama Lacy's not here to care," I snap, more to myself than to my sister, and I shove my door open, letting the snow in.

"She can still see you," Zany says. "She still knows if you're hitting me." She sounds tired as she shoves her door open, too.

"She cannot," I argue. "She can't see us or she'd find a way to help us . . . fix stuff."

"Don't be stupid." Her voice is starting to sound mad. "Of course she can't fix everything. She's not here anymore, but that doesn't mean she can't see us. I know she's still watching us and she can hear us. She can hear you saying she can't."

"No she can't!"

"Yes, she can, jerk!" I am pleased when Zany sinks to my level.

"Well, if she can, then she just heard you call me a jerk!" I'm triumphant.

Zany growls wordlessly and heads off into the snow. I scramble to follow, but it takes a minute to get Haberdashery to stay in the truck. By the time I'm free to run after her, Zany is several feet away, jogging through the gray snow. Fear spikes in me. It's so lonely out here. Zany might drive me crazy, but I don't want to be away from her.

"What are you doing?" I shout, shivering as the wet snow soaks through my robe.

"Looking for the wiper!" Zany hollers. She's holding her hands above her eyes to keep the snow out so she can scan the ground. "Where is it?"

"You're not going to find it!"

"I have to! We can't wait out the snowstorm!"

"You can't find it!" I repeat.

"I have to!" She's screaming, I'm not sure if it's because she's upset or because it's hard to hear each other, but she's screaming and it scares me even more.

"Use the other one!" I holler, even though it's a silly thing to say.

"But it's on the wrong side!"

"Well, move it!" Even sillier, but what else can we do?

"You can't move a wiper!"

My heart's pounding. I'm terrified that if she gets out of sight, I'll never find her again. "Wait!" I shout, pushing forward through the snow. She doesn't say anything, but she waits. I catch up, and in my hurry to reach her, I can't stop. I barrel into her hard enough to make her stumble. "Let's try, at least!" Still arguing to fix the wiper, but all the while holding her hand.

"Hey, you're crushing my fingers." Then, "Geez, Fella, you're squeezing my hand to death. What's the matter? Are you scared?"

"No!" I hear tears in my voice. My heart's still pounding. I'm more scared of being left alone than I was of the truck sliding in the snow. "You just shouldn't leave me alone by the road, that's all!"

"Shoot, I'm sorry." She walks with me toward the truck, catching her breath. "I'm sorry. I didn't mean to scare you."

I'm breathing hard, too. It's slow work, slipping and sliding along the edge of the interstate in a snowstorm. I'm not about to admit how frightened I got when she walked away and have Zany call me a baby for the next six months. "It's okay."

A quick search of Adam's truck reveals a giant

stuffed panda—"I'll have to ask him about that later,"
Zany mutters—and about a million fast-food wrappers
under the topper over the truck bed. There are three
half-used rolls of duct tape and a flashlight with weak
batteries. It flickers and dims, but it's something.

Through the snow, Zany studies the broken edge of
the windshield wiper. I wiggle back and forth from foot
to foot, trying not to freeze to death on the spot.

"Looks like it broke off about an inch above where it
hooks on. How in the world did he manage to break his
windshield wiper there?"

I walk around to the passenger side, glance at Zany's
wiper and then mine, and begin working to snap it off the
same length.

"Hey, what are you doing? Fella, whoa! Don't break
off the only wiper we've got!"

An eighteen-wheeler blasts past, splashing us both
with slushy water, and we screech and duck away. Once
it's gone, I stand again. "What's the difference?" I point
out. "You can't drive with the left one missing anyway!
What do you need the right one for?"

She stares at me for a minute, a stare that is every
bit Mama Shannon's *Bedtime is when I say it is, not when
you say it is, young lady* stare. But then her face changes
and she shrugs.

162

"I guess you've got a point, Light Bulb!"

Twenty minutes and a lot of swearing from Zany later, she's duct-taped the newly broken wiper to the nub left over on the driver's side. She's also taped my fingers to the wiper three times. Once I'm unstuck, we dash for the dryness of the truck's cab, bringing the snowstorm in with us. Haberdashery makes a disapproving noise and scoots toward the center of the seat, the only dry spot.

Back in the truck, we have to stop being numb before we can start warming up, so it feels like we get colder for a while before we get warmer. It takes ages before either one of us can speak around our chattering teeth. Zany blasts the weak heater till I start to feel my toes again.

"Did *you* know how hard it is to use duct tape in wet weather?" she breathes at last.

I shrug. Give her a half smile. "It stuck to my fingers all right."

She rolls her eyes at me, but she grins, too. We sit in the car awhile longer, feeling squishy and cold and sort of proud of ourselves, before Zany pulls us back onto the road, heading toward a distant streak of light beginning to glow through the snow clouds. It's barely a glimmer, but I think it might be the sun.

chapter
19

"**We're stopping?**" I sit up straighter when Zany aims the car toward another gas station. We're both shivering steadily now, even with the truck heat on.

"We can dry off under the hand dryers," she says. Then reveals her true reason: "Plus, I need coffee."

The gas station isn't a chain. It's a small country store that has a creepy feel about it, and I don't know if I can trust that it's clean.

Inside, a woman dozes behind the counter next to the cigarette shelf. She's propped crooked on a tall stool with a ripped seat.

"Is she going to fall?" I ask out of the corner of my

mouth at Zany. Zany nudges me, because we can't help giggling. Then she clears her throat noisily to wake the lady, even though I can tell she's worried the lady might recognize us from the news.

"Welcome to Smart Stop," the woman says without opening her eyes, but I notice she does balance herself a little more squarely on the stool. "Let me know, I can help you with something." She leaves out *if*, as if the strain of that one word would be enough to wear her out completely.

"No, thanks," Zany says. "We're just here for the bathroom and coffee."

"Well, you'll need my help after all, then. Bathroom code is seven-one-seven and you gotta pay a dime."

Zany stares at her with guilt on her face, but the lady's eyes stay closed. I'm dancing in place. I shouldn't have gulped that whole soda at the Waffle House.

I'm glad this one has an indoor bathroom, not like the one in Wytheville. It's not as filthy, either, and the mirror isn't cracked, we find after inserting a dime into the slot on the door and punching in the code. In the mirror, I'm amazed at the reflection of two wet, worn-out girls.

"Wow, do we look pretty right now," Zany says with

a crooked grin. "Thank goodness we didn't get soaked till after we dropped off Adam."

"Of course you'd think that," I say. "You have to look pretty for a thief!"

She turns on the hand dryer, the noise saving her from having to answer for a minute. Hot air blasts out and we take turns huddling under the fan, trying to dry off. I know the air is hot, but it feels cold rushing at my wet skin and drippy clothes. I realize that unless we stay here all morning, the most I can hope for is that my clothes and hair will be a little less drippy.

When the hand dryer shuts off, I ask, "So what *is* it about Adam?"

"Huh?" She's still fixing herself up in the mirror, only half listening.

"Adam. You've known him, like—what, eight hours? Less? Why do you like him?"

"Who says I like him?"

"Well, you were kissing him."

She spins to look at me. "Spy."

"I'm not a spy! You were kissing him right out in the open, right out in the truck! Where anybody could see you! And you don't even know him!"

"I do, sort of."

"No, you don't!"

"Well, we're going through the same thing."

"How do you know? He's a total stranger. How do you know he's not making everything up just to get away with stealing our stuff?" Though I know he isn't making things up. You can't fake the things he said on the phone, or the voice he said them in.

She rolls her eyes. "We're the thieves now, don't forget."

"You didn't answer me." I really want to know. I can't figure out what it is about a person that makes them so interesting to another person. It's a little bit scary, thinking about liking somebody outside my family so much that my life would be sad without them. I already have enough people right here in my own family to lose without adding anybody else.

"Didn't answer what?" Zany asks. She's turned and is leaning against the sink, drawing patterns on the damp floor tiles with the toe of her boot.

"Why do you like Adam?"

"I don't know." She shrugs. "It's been . . . it's been a long time since I've liked anything. Since I've been anything except sad." She grins sideways at me. "And he *is* cute. And he makes me feel, God, Fella, I don't know. Just *something*. Besides sad, for a minute."

"Oh." I wonder what I have in my life that makes

me feel something besides sad for a minute. There's Haberdashery (who makes me feel annoyed but also like I want to snuggle). There's Zany (who makes me want to tear my hair out but also makes me feel like I'm home after a long trip). There's not much else. "Oh," I say again.

"Come on. We need to get coffee and get on the road." She leads me out into the gas station and fills a coffee cup. Then another.

"I need you to stay awake with me," she explains, dumping sugar packet after sugar packet into the cups. After pouring in creamer, she presses one warm Styrofoam cup into my hands. "Drink this."

I take a cautious sniff. The smell of coffee brings back long talks with Mama Shannon, and the thought of her makes my stomach swim with guilt. Right now, our mama is worried about us, not knowing where we are or if we're okay. Mama Shannon has been different ever since Mama Lacy died—no games of kickball in the yard, no laughs, no bad jokes or rowdy laughter. It didn't use to be like her to worry, which somehow makes it worse that we're making her do it now.

In the truck, I look at the gas station through the blurry side of the windshield. Zany has hopped back out to throw away the Twinkies trash we've piled up at our stops, plus some of the junk that was already littering Adam's truck. I don't understand how Zany can find Adam cute when he keeps his dad's truck such a mess, but it doesn't seem to faze her. She scoops out a couple of McDonald's bags, much to the dismay of Haberdashery, who is waking up enough to scavenge.

"Stop it, you pig," she says. "This is Adam's stuff." Her voice sounds all googly on the word *Adam*. I can't be mad at her for wanting to feel something other than sad, but I can still think it's gross. "Anyway, we brought you something." She peels back the top of the tin of food we bought for him. He dives into it with such fury that I have to reach out to steady the can so he doesn't shove it off the seat. It takes him less than a minute to eat the whole meal, which makes me feel better about his health. He must be okay if he can still be a pig.

Haberdashery starts to whimper just as Zany starts the engine.

"Uh-oh. Hang on." I recognize this whimper because I've made the same sound several times on this trip. I start digging around for a leash and finally think to tear off a long strip of duct tape and roll it longwise into a cord. Zany watches with interest.

"What are you doing?"

"It's a leash!" I'm surprised she can't tell. I tie one

end of the tape around the ring on Haberdashery's collar, and I hang on to the other end tightly. "This dumb dog is not going to run off again!" But I scratch between his ears while I say it so he doesn't think I actually mean the dumb part.

"Well, hurry up, okay? I'm freezing." Zany stays in the truck to wait.

"I don't know how you think me hurrying is going to help you warm up," I grumble, but I tug Haberdashery faster all the same.

There's barely any grass outside the gas station, and I have to walk Haberdashery all the way around the building to find a spot he'll use for the bathroom. It's creepy back here, gray and lonely. The only people I see are truckers walking to and from the big-rig parking lot on the other side of a fence.

"Come on," I mutter. "Do your business." But the poodle thinks he's got to sniff every single blade of grass before he decides on one to use as his bathroom. He also wants to sample the water out of every puddle.

It seems darker back here. I don't like being close to so many parked cars, grim and shadowed. I can't tell whether or not there are people inside them. I'm relieved when Haberdashery finishes what he's doing. As I tug him back around the corner of the gas station, I can see Zany sitting in the truck, phone to her ear. My stomach flip-flops and I tug Haberdashery to the truck. My heart starts to pound. I don't want Adam to be calling with bad news. I know it has to be Adam. If it were Mama Shannon, I'm not sure she'd answer for fear of being talked into coming home.

"Is everything okay?" I ask, breathless, as I yank the door open. "Is Adam's dad okay?"

Zany shushes me with a wave of her hand. "I know," she says into the phone. Another pause. "I know, I really do."

My heart thumps. "Did he go in? Did he get to talk to him?"

She covers the receiver. "Fella, hush!"

"Did he die?"

"Fella!" she shouts, but she puts the phone to her ear for a minute and then hands it to me. "He wants to talk to you."

I tug Haberdashery into the truck and close the door behind us. "Adam?"

"Hey. It's okay, my dad—he's still here. I didn't mean to scare you."

I slump against the seat and take several deep breaths. "Oh!" My eyes still prickle. "Okay. Did you talk to him?" My voice comes out sounding like a little kid's, and I squeeze my eyes shut to keep from crying.

"I will," he says. "I will, but—not yet. Let me talk to your sister again, okay?"

I hand her the phone and climb back out of the truck to let her talk. I wander into the gas station. The only sound is the TV behind the counter, with the end of some early-morning infomercial just going off the air.

A teaser comes on for the Sunday-morning news and I see my face as the bell jingles on the door.

"Oh—" Zany stops just behind me. Then tugs my arm. "Fella. Come on."

But she's staring at what I'm staring at, and neither one of us moves toward the door. It's Mama Shannon. And it's Mrs. Madison. Both of them together on the news.

The sleepy woman on her stool isn't paying attention. She hasn't looked at the TV the whole time I've been in here. Still, I feel like she's going to look up at any moment and then it will all be over. The police will be called and we'll be sent straight to jail for truck theft and poodlenapping and whatever else we've done tonight that is an actual crime.

"Come on," Zany says again, starting to move. "We have to go."

But I can't take my eyes off my two family members on TV. The last time I saw them together for any length

172

of time, they were in a courtroom, fighting over me. I think about how mad I've been at both of them ever since, how I've been furious at Mrs. Madison for taking me away and at Mama Shannon for not making it better somehow.

Standing here looking at their worried faces on the screen, I feel this sinking in my heart. They both wanted me. They both want me still and are worried enough about me and Zany to ignore how much they dislike each other as they work together to find us.

"Fella." Zany takes my hand in hers, laces her fingers through mine. Pulls. "We have to go. We have to go now." She's looking toward the counter, where the clerk has just turned to focus on the TV. "Come on. Come *on!*"

I do. As we leave, I hear Haberdashery's name.

"They're traveling with a poodle," Mrs. Madison's saying. "He's eight years old, about twelve pounds. He is very special to me—"

The door closes behind us, cutting off the rest of her words. Zany hurries me toward the truck and we pile in so quickly that Haberdashery squeaks. I end up sitting on Adam's phone and I squirm to grab it and stick it in my pocket.

"You're famous," I tell Haberdashery. Zany hits the gas a little too hard and the truck squeaks forward, spitting gravel into the parking lot behind us. She gets us smoothed out and steady on the road, heading for the interstate. I'm relieved we've escaped, but fear starts to creep in as Zany aims for the on-ramp, pushing the pedal down, faster, then faster still. We pop up onto the interstate so suddenly that a delivery van has to veer out of our path. The sound of his horn sideswipes us, but luckily that's the only thing that does.

I glance over at Zany to see what on earth is going through her mind. She's driving like a madwoman. But she doesn't look concerned, just distracted and upset.

"I hate her," she mutters.

"What are you talking about?"

"Moaning about her poodle all over TV. Doesn't she remember she's got granddaughters?" Something in me feels off center. Then a little more when Zany says, louder, stomping on the gas, "I really hate that lady!"

My eyes sting like maybe I'm going to start crying, except I don't know why. I already know Zany hates Mrs. Madison. Mama Shannon probably does, too. I think I'm also supposed to hate her, after everything she's done. Cutting our family out of her life. Stealing me from Mama Shannon.

But . . .

Miles go by to the sound of Zany's breathing, the air

in the truck growing still as my sister slowly unwinds. It's several minutes before I speak.

"There's a picture on Mrs. Madison's dresser," I tell Zany, not completely sure why I'm telling her, except that I want her to crawl into my thoughts with me and figure out which direction they're supposed to go next.

"Of her best friend, the devil?" Zany asks. Her voice isn't as mad as it was before.

"No!"

"Of her ugly, stupid poodle?"

I give Haberdashery a squeeze. "No! Stop it, Zany!"

She glances at me and the whole truck shimmies. "Why should I?"

I'm too frustrated now to answer, and I turn and look out the windshield instead, watching drops of melted snow blow down the window. They pick up speed halfway down and roll, roll, and then, no matter how carefully I watch them, they disappear and I can't find them again.

"What's the picture of?" Zany asks after a minute.

"Nothing." I'm sulking now. Can't help it. It's easier than tearing apart these feelings.

She lets out a short sigh. "Fella—" Her voice is high with anxiety and frustration. It isn't until we've passed a few more mile markers that she manages to bring it back down to calm.

"Fella," she says again, this time sounding more like Mama Lacy than herself, practical and soothing, and older than sixteen. "What's the picture of, hmm?"

I chew my lip a minute. I only mean to point out that Mrs. Madison isn't hateful, that she does have a loving side to her.

"It's me," I mumble. Now that I'm saying it, it feels weird. Not as good as I thought it would sound.

Zany changes lanes to get around a slow trucker. Back in our own lane a minute later, she asks, "Just you?"

Which is, of course, what feels weird about it. "Yes," I say in a tiny voice. I'm ashamed about feeling good that I've got Mrs. Madison when Zany doesn't. After all, we both have Granny Culvert, even though she's far away.

"Just you," Zany says again, soft. "You know, Fella, now that I think about it? I really hate that woman."

I don't know whether I agree or disagree. Sort of both.

chapter
20

I ought not to be able to recognize the road at the end of Tennessee, but my breath quickens anyway and I know we're about to cross into North Carolina. I almost sense a change in the air, like it's vibrating. Like it's thick with the memories I lost along the road five years ago, memories I'll pick up as we cross back into the state. It might be the air freshener Zany bought at the last gas station, but I imagine I can smell piney woods and sweet red earth and clean raindrops.

For the first time, I feel something other than dread at the thought of reaching Asheville.

Zany must not feel the same way, because she pulls over at yet another gas station. We keep stopping at gas stations, even though we're down to the last few pennies in our pockets. It's a terrible risk, to keep stopping. Zany mentions it every time she pulls off the road. We're going to get caught. But we're so tired and the road is the same all the time. We need the stops to stay awake.

She rolls us past the pumps and parks outside the glass doors. Inside I see a cashier watching a tiny TV in the corner. It's mid-morning after a very long night, and his head looks like it's starting to bob. I know how he feels.

I don't make any move to get out of the truck. Zany doesn't, either. The brass urn and the bandaged poodle sit between us on the seat.

"Not too much longer," Zany says. I don't answer. Above the mountains, the sun is just visible. According to the clock hanging on the wall beside the TV, it's after eight. We're drawing closer and closer to the time when I'll have to let go of Mama Lacy. I want to reach over and pick up the urn, but when I try, I find the seat empty. Zany's beat me to it. She's holding the urn and she's got her face turned away, out the window. I feel left out and awkward. I think I should reach toward her, but I don't.

After a minute, Zany turns back toward me. She smiles kind of soft and it doesn't reach her eyes. She looks like Adam did in Wytheville when he said he wasn't ready. But there's no twenty-four-hour department store here and anyways that isn't what we need.

I don't know what we need. Don't know if anything will ever fill the gap left by what we don't have.

"You going in?" I ask Zany, nodding toward the gas station.

She shakes her head. "You?"

"Nah."

Zany starts the truck and we back out. I watch sleepy houses slip by as we drift onto the interstate, the only car out at this hour that's heading up the mountain.

chapter
21

The speed limit drops to sixty-five. Then sixty. Then fifty-five. By the time we reach the top of the first mountain, we're going forty-five and the morning fog is so thick, I can't even tell we're on a mountain. Which means I can't tell where the edge is, either.

"Zany . . . ," I breathe. I'm terrified we're going to drive right over the edge of the mountain in this fog, and not even know until we're on the way down.

"Relax," Zany demands, her teeth clenched. I know my sister well enough to know what she means is, *Shut up and don't bother me*. I'm nervous enough I want to keep talking, but I also don't want to do anything that might startle Zany and distract her from the road. I rock my armload of poodle and urn, humming under my breath. After a while,

I realize it's the song from the jukebox, the one our whole family used to sing together. *The sound of children playing / And the sound of people saying, I love you . . .*

"Relax," she says again. I think this time she might be talking to herself.

It isn't until a graveyard looms at the side of the road that I realize it.

"Zany, have you noticed we're the only ones on the road?" I worry the other drivers know something we don't, that maybe there's a storm coming, or a wreck up ahead, or some other disaster lying in wait.

Zany glances in her mirrors and at the white dashed line stretching away in front of us.

"I did notice that," she says faintly. "It's a good thing, too. Hard to see each other in this fog." As if this reminds her, she flips on the emergency flashers to warn motorists traveling faster that we're here in the slow lane. The orange lights splash on the fog, then disappear. Splash, disappear. Splash, disappear.

"Yeah," I echo. "Good." I think about how if we break down, it will be an hour before somebody finds us. I wonder if the headlights will stay on if that happens. I'm glad to see the graveyard fade away behind us in the fog. But just because it's out of sight doesn't mean I don't know it's still there. I squeeze Haberdashery a little tighter.

I'm relieved when we start back down the mountain. Now the drop-off is far away, across the empty lanes that head back in the other direction. On my side there are rocky cliffs leading up to the trees. They're cut square and I can see them even through the fog.

I've started to relax, settling down into the warmth of the truck, when there's this whirring, thumping noise and I feel like I'm falling. My arms fly out, looking for Mama Lacy, and instead they find Haberdashery, who is so frightened by the commotion that he tries to climb me like I'm a tree. I steady him.

"What—?" I shout.

"It's okay," Zany says in a scared voice that lets me know it is not at all okay. "We're okay!" She eases the failing truck onto the shoulder and shuts off the engine. We both sit breathing heavy for a minute.

"What happened?" I ask when I've got my breath caught enough to speak.

"I . . . I think we got a flat." Zany waits for a coal truck to pass, then gets out of the truck and circles around. The fog is starting to give way to a cold drizzle. I open my door in time to hear her swear, and then I see why. The right front tire is completely flat and sitting on the rim.

Zany deflates like the tire, leaning against the truck and laying her head on the filthy hood. She closes her

182

eyes for a minute. "I'm so tired," she says. Then, "I'll bet there's no spare." She goes to the back and peers under the topper. "Well, he's got one," she hollers, "but it's flat!"

My heart's still racing and I sink onto the shoulder of the road, where it meets the grass. Right away, I feel icy water soaking my clothes. Zany blows air out through her lips in frustration. "We're going to have to start walking. I don't know what else to do."

I look down the long highway, deserted now in both directions. Behind us the road disappears upward in the drizzle. Below us, I can only see a few feet of mountain before the thick fog swallows the road. Once in a while, a giant coal truck blasts past, but I haven't seen a regular car since the last gas station.

"I'm not sure that's a good idea," I say.

"And what's your idea? Sit here till somebody happens across us, and hope they won't call the cops?"

"Call! We can call someone."

"Who?"

I run through the list—Mama Shannon? Mrs. Madison? The police? I can't say any of them to Zany.

"We have to walk," she says again.

"But we can't leave the truck. Adam needs it back in the morning."

I see the battle crossing her face. See her weighing

183

our options. Finally, she steels her gaze and steadies her chin. "Sure we can," she says, and starts walking.

"Wait up," I holler after her. "I've got to get Haberdashery! And Mama Lacy!"

She stops dead. "Jesus, I almost left without them. I'm so tired." She runs a hand down her face.

"Maybe we should sit down a little while."

"No, if I sit down, I'm not going to get back up. We need to keep moving." She doesn't sound sure, and I don't like it. Zany is supposed to know what to do.

I stumble back to the truck, slipping on gravel, and I scoop up Haberdashery and hand Mama Lacy's ashes to Zany. The poodle tucks his face under my elbow. With my free hand I check to make sure we've got the phone. At least we'll be able to call Adam and tell him about his truck. If we can get up the nerve.

"I bet you wish you didn't sneak out with us now, don't you?" I murmur at the poodle when he whimpers. But I can't hate him when he's injured, so I pet his curly ears and he wags his nubby tail.

"Zany, are you sure about this?" I ask.

She starts walking without saying anything.

"Zany—hey. Wait up."

But she doesn't, and she won't look at me, even when I trot to catch up with her, Haberdashery heavy in my arms. She turns her face away, and I hear a sound like a sniffle. My stomach starts to hurt.

"Are you crying?"

"Be quiet."

Zany never cries, and when she does, she just wants to be left alone, but there's no way for me to leave her alone out here.

"But—but are you?"

"Shush." She most definitely is crying.

I don't know what to say. I've been away from Zany too long. During most of the time I was crying for Mama Lacy, I wasn't anywhere near Zany. Now it occurs to me that the same is true in reverse, that Zany has been off somewhere alone, or with Mama Shannon, crying for Mama Lacy without me knowing anything about it.

"You know we can't walk there, right?" I ask in the most gentle voice I can figure out how to use.

"If you want to do something, just decide to," she says, and I realize she's quoting Mama Shannon.

"Zany, why is it *so* important that we do this? That we make it there today? We can go another day. It doesn't have to be her birthday."

"She had a deadline," Zany says. "Don't you remember? She wanted to have it all over and done. The cancer and all. She wanted to make it back to Asheville, back to our life, before she turned forty." Zany sniffles. "Well, she's turning forty. Or anyway, she would be. And she's going to get there. She decided to. If you decide to, you can do anything."

"Except stay together."

I hear Zany breathe in like something hurts. She doesn't speak, so I keep going.

"Mama Lacy decided to live and it didn't work. I decided to stay with you and Mama Shannon, but it didn't work. Why do you think we can make this work, Zoey Grace?"

I hear her breathe in again. Hear her sniffle. But her answer never comes. We walk along the shoulder in silence, stepping as far off the road as we can get when the coal trucks rush past. I feel the dog tense in my arms. One time, Zany sees a police car going the opposite direction and she drags me behind the guard-rail to hide. Almost right away, a sharp rock slides into my sneaker.

"I wish you'd worn real shoes," Zany says when she notices me limping. "This is probably child abuse. I could probably go to jail for letting you do this." Her voice still sounds like she's maybe crying a little bit.

"I'm not a little kid," I protest. "I'm fine. These shoes are fine." I try not to let her see me limp after that.

We pass a mile marker that says 1 and I try to remember how the mile markers work. I know they count up or down from the border of a state. I don't know how far away Asheville is from the border, so it doesn't make a whole lot of difference to me, but I do know we're not going to be able to walk the whole way. Still I plod after Zany. The poodle gets heavier and my arms ache.

It seems like hours and hours pass. I'm panting and limping and complaining loudly about the stitch in my side and how thirsty I am and how we forgot our Twinkies in Adam's truck, and then we pass a mile marker sign that says 2 and I sit down in a heap.

"We've only gone a mile?" I wail.

"Fella!" Zany throws up her free hand in frustration. "Are you going to moan and groan the whole way? Because if so, can you walk on the other side of the road? I'm sick of listening to it!"

"But this dog is heavy! And I'm *starving*!" Well, not exactly starving. But I'm starting to get hungry, and so is the poodle.

"I've got a little change in my pocket," Zany says. "Can't you make it to the rest area?"

The mention of a rest area interests me, and I let my sister pull me to my feet. "Where's there a rest area?" I ask suspiciously, squinting ahead.

"It's somewhere on the mountain," she says.

"Well, that's specific." But I follow her. We've passed another mile marker before the exit finally comes into view through the fog.

At the rest area, I make a beeline for the snack machines. Zany heads for the bathroom. While she's gone, I put Haberdashery down on his three good legs, and I hold the end of his duct-tape leash so he can't run off and cause any more trouble.

There are signs pointing to a scenic overlook and I'm thinking how cool it would be to pop up and look over the mountains with their fog. Maybe from up there we'll be able to see Asheville. Maybe we're almost home.

I wait and wait for Zany, but she doesn't come out. When I go into the building after her, I think she's studying the giant map on the wall, but she turns out to be listening to the radio, which is going on about two missing kids who sound awfully familiar. The reception is spotty, maybe because of the rain. I hear the words *runaway* and *custody*. A minute later, I hear *poodle*, and I tug on Zany's arm.

"We should keep moving, don't you think?"

She nods.

I lead her out of the building and toward the scenic

overlook, thinking maybe from there we can see if any police cars are after us. She doesn't ask where we're going, just follows me, and by the time we're halfway there, she's in the lead. My nose and my ears and my toes are so cold they ache, and my breath is coming out in my own little puffs of fog.

At the top of the steep trail is a wooden platform surrounded by a tall railing. There's a sign here, but I don't read it. Instead I climb onto the railing and sit. Below my dangling feet, Haberdashery whines. Zany leans next to me and we gaze at what is supposed to be a breathtaking view of the mountains.

All I see is fog.

"I think we're alone," Zany says.

I nod. "I think we're all alone in the whole world."

We let the words get soaked up by the heavy fog and the forest. But it doesn't feel like the words are disappearing. It feels like they're going someplace. I get shivers and I feel like something strange is happening. I think of the letter back home in my treasure box, the one in Mama Lacy's neat handwriting, which got messier toward the end.

"Do you really think Mama Lacy can hear us when we talk to her?" I ask, half hoping the fog will eat up my voice before my pathetic question makes it to Zany's ears.

No such luck. Zany turns to look at me.

"I think she can hear everything we say, whether we're talking to her or not."

It's weird then that she's my sister and we're still so different. She's got this faith in the universe, that it can get messages to our dead mama, that a birthday present still matters even if the person you're giving it to is never going to have another birthday. And me, I'm trying to see through the fog to pick out the individual water droplets. I can't leave anything alone and I can't let anything just be magic. I have to pick it apart until I know how it works. I can't see how anybody can hear us but each other, least of all Mama Lacy.

"Come on," Zany says, jerking her chin back toward the road. "We got a long way to go yet, Fella."

I don't answer. I just quietly follow her down the trail. Right before we get out of sight of the overlook, I turn and whisper.

"Mama Lacy? Can you hear me?"

I hear wind in the leaves and a truck whooshing down the interstate, but nobody answers.

chapter
22

At the base of the overlook trail,
Zany stops walking so fast I smack into her nose-first.
My feet slide and I stomp in frustration.

"What are—"

That's as far as I get before Zany spins around and
slaps a hand over my mouth. I'm so startled I step backward too quickly and we both go tumbling into the
woods in a heap.

I'm all set to let loose screaming at my crazy sister,
when I hear a familiar voice cutting through the fog.

"I honestly don't see why you have to stop at every
gas station and rest stop! You know where they're going!
You know they're probably already there!"

"Pipe down!" Mama Shannon's voice sounds the

way it always does when she's dealing with Mrs. Madison—frazzled to the breaking point, like a rope swing wearing through. Any minute she's going to crack and start screeching at Mrs. Madison the way I sometimes do with Zany.

"No, young lady," Mrs. Madison trills, "I will not, as you so gracefully request, 'pipe down.' I'm just as concerned about my granddaughter as you are and my advice is just as valid—if not more so. You're hysterical. And you still haven't answered my question. Why do you insist on stopping at every gas station and rest area to wave a picture in people's faces when you know the girls are probably right up ahead in that city you all seem to like so much?"

"Because!" I have not ventured to stand up and get a look, but Mama Shannon's voice is getting farther away. "They left the car in Virginia! There's no way they made it to Asheville already. And if some trucker or somebody on this road picked them up, I want to know where they are and if they're safe!" Her voice cracks on the word *safe*, and Zany squeezes my hand. "I can't pass up a stop where the girls might be sitting, waiting to be rescued! And you have *two* granddaughters!"

I should have known she hadn't missed that last part. My stomach aches with guilt. I think maybe I should have been reminding Mrs. Madison of Zany all along. Zany would have, if she had been in my shoes. But Zany never seems to have trouble finding her courage. She's driven this whole trip, and I don't just mean that she's driven the truck. It was all her idea, and I've been trying to pull her back the whole time. I worm my hand out of hers, not feeling like I deserve the comfort, but she picks it up again and I'm glad.

When Mama Shannon's and Mrs. Madison's voices get distant enough that I know they can't see us where we are, I stand slowly. Zany pulls me back and goes ahead of me, which makes sense since she's wearing black instead of shimmery pink. I'm surprised to see Mrs. Madison's shiny, rarely used car outside its garage. It isn't so shiny now that it's coated in road salt.

"I can't believe they teamed up," Zany marvels.

"Yeah, well, Mrs. Madison doesn't drive. She'd have needed Mama Shannon to take care of that part. And Mama Shannon didn't have a car, since we stole it and broke it, so I guess—"

"Yeah, I get it, I'm just saying." Zany's keeping her voice low even though both grown-ups have gone inside the bathrooms.

"Should we tell them we're here?" I ask Zany. I'm really hoping she'll say yes. They can talk her out of scattering Mama Lacy's ashes in Asheville. They can talk some sense into her where I can't.

Or maybe I'm hoping they can talk me into it. I'm worried it might be the right thing to do.

Zany starts shaking her head. Before she says anything, I run after my mother and grandmother. Zany catches up just as I reach the map on the wall outside the bathroom doors. She pulls me back and puts a finger to her lips, a fierce expression demanding that I stop.

"They'll hear you!" she whispers.

But it immediately becomes apparent that they're not going to hear us. They still haven't stopped arguing.

"Maybe if your car would go faster than fifty-five," Mama Shannon is saying.

"Your car is on the shoulder of the highway in Virginia, so I wouldn't be quick to judge. We wouldn't even be here without my car."

"We wouldn't even be here," Mama Shannon shoots back, "if you hadn't kidnapped my daughter."

"You're being dramatic."

"Well, if I still had both the girls and they wanted to go to Asheville for Lacy's birthday, I would have found a way to take them. They wouldn't have had to sneak. If they were both still with me, they would have told me their plan. They must have known I wouldn't take them, wouldn't risk losing what little time I do have with Fella by taking her and having you report me as kidnapping her."

Mrs. Madison makes the noise that she always makes when her gardening club ladies get ready to leave, like it's a real shame to see them go. "It's sad," she says, "to see you lose your head so completely. You're not making any sense."

"Even though you did it legally, through the court, you know it was wrong to take Fella," Mama Shannon says. She seems to have been saving up her words for a long time. "Lacy and I were raising the girls together. We were a family. It doesn't matter what the law says. It doesn't matter we weren't allowed to get married or to adopt each other's kids. We *chose* our family and we *built* our family and you don't have to agree with Lacy's choices, but you ought to respect them, especially since she isn't here to defend herself."

"And whose fault is that?" Mrs. Madison asks, and then we all go quiet. Zany squeezes my fingers in hers. Neither of us can quite catch our breath after what we've just heard.

Mrs. Madison does something then that I've never before heard her do. She backpedals. "That isn't exactly what I meant to say." But it's too late. Her accusation hangs in the air like the dark clouds that have followed us all the way to North Carolina.

"And what exactly did you mean by 'that isn't exactly what you meant to say'?" Mama Shannon says like she can't quite find her air.

"I didn't mean to say that," Mrs. Madison says. "I'm worried, that's all."

"Yeah," says Zany. "About your poodle."

Too late, she realizes she's spoken loud enough to be heard. The door swings open so quickly that we have to step back out of the way. Both the grown-ups start talking at once and Zany moans in dismay. We've been caught.

chapter
23

"Lord God above." Mrs. Madison clasps her hands in front of her as if she's praying. Beside her, Mama Shannon doesn't seem to know what to do with her body. She steps forward, stops. She closes her eyes and lets out this shaky, forceful breath. Her fingertips press against her lips, and she has to start three times before she can make words come out.

"Are you girls all right?" she asks at last, in a voice hoarse with worry. I've never seen her look quite like she does right now. Her face is pinched tight, looking so much like Zany's when she's mad. Both of them have freckles that stand out against their pale skin. Both of them have faces that look more natural with a smile than a frown. Mama Shannon's voice wavers. "You haven't been hurt?"

"We're fine," Zany says.

"We're fine," I echo.

"How long have you been hiding out here, letting us look for you?" Mama Shannon demands. I remember how sometimes when I get scared, it makes me get mad, so I try not to be upset at the anger in my mother's voice.

"We just walked this far because Adam's truck got a flat," Zany says.

"Who's Adam?" Mama Shannon is quick to ask.

"He's the guy who stole Mama Lacy," I jump in, "but he gave her back when he realized what she was. And your car was overheating plus anyway the police found it, so Adam gave us a ride, and then we stole his truck."

"You rode with a stranger?" Mrs. Madison shrieks, as if we have just announced that we rode with a convicted murderer. This is the first attention she's paid to us, as she has been kneeling in front of Haberdashery, exploring every inch of him and letting him lick her face.

"He was going the right direction," Zany says.

"Asheville," Mama Shannon confirms. "Yeah, I put that together when the vet called from over Wytheville way and then the cop saw you down near Bristol."

"Who called you?"

"The *police* called me, Ophelia. The police called to keep me up to date. They know I'm out on the road following you. They told me not to, but . . ." She shakes her head back and forth, back and forth. "I knew where you were going, so I started after you. Stopped here and there to show your picture to a few people, but I didn't know where to start. You could have been killed!"

"We're fine, Mama," Zany says. "We were going to be home before you even woke up, but . . ." She waves a hand in the air because there is no way to explain in words all the things that went wrong with that plan.

Mama Shannon taps her fingers together for a minute and then she's hugging us so tightly I can't breathe. She's got one arm around Zany and the other around me and my face is pressed to her chest. I've never felt her hold on so tight before, and I reach to hold on just as tightly. My throat clogs with tears. I didn't realize until I had a Mama Shannon hug how badly I'd needed one.

We don't talk again until we're in the car, Mrs. Madison clinging to a wriggling Haberdashery and fussing over his injuries. Without him, my arms feel empty. I almost wish Zany would give me back the urn, but she's cradling it in both hands. The rest area is only available to eastbound cars, so we have to keep going toward Asheville, though Mama Shannon makes it clear we'll be turning around as soon as we find an exit.

"Once I called Joanie and she told me the ashes were gone, I knew what you were doing." Her voice is low, almost dangerously angry. But I can't help asking.

"Who's Joanie?"

All three of my family members in the car swivel to stare at me, until I feel my face get red because the answer must be obvious to everybody else.

"Joan Madison," Mrs. Madison says, extending her hand. "Pleasure to meet you."

"Oh." I sulk, feeling stupid. How should I know my grandmother's first name when nobody ever calls her by it?

But Mama Shannon still isn't done. She keeps going with a voice that gets slower and more serious with every word.

"You were going to scatter my wife's ashes without me. Do you not—do you not understand how that's wrong? Do you not understand how you can't do that to a person? I tried to raise you girls to be more thoughtful than that, and I know Lacy did better than me at raising you that way. So how can you not think about me? Waking up to find out that you're gone. Waking up and finding Lacy gone . . . forever . . . again . . ." Her voice breaks and I hear her crying. She sounds less like a mom right now than I have ever heard. I want to crawl into the front seat and hug her again, but this isn't like I've stayed up past bedtime or made a failing grade on a spelling test. This isn't something I can fix with a hug. I sneak closer to Zany, but she doesn't look like she knows what to do, either.

Then Mama Shannon's mom voice snaps back on at full volume. "And, Zoey Grace, I don't know what you thought you were doing, dragging your sister along! You're old enough to know how dangerous the road is! Riding with a stranger! Who is this Adam? How did you know he wouldn't hurt you?" Her voice shakes so hard my hands start to shake, too. "You didn't know who he was. He could have been anybody!"

"He was nice, Mama," I try, but she talks over me.

"He could have killed you, Zany, or he could have killed your sister! And the kinds of people who eat at the Waffle House in the middle of the night?"

"It was the police, Mama, that's who ate at the Waffle House in the middle of the night."

"It could have been *anyone*! Any place you stopped, you could have been *killed*!"

Zany's wilting before my eyes. Drawing her feet up

201

on the seat so her chin rests on her knees. Looping her arms around her legs. "I know it."

"I don't think you do, or you wouldn't have done it!"

"No, I do. I was just—I was desperate. It's her birthday tomorrow—today. And she won't get any older. And she had that deadline. I needed to do something."

Mama Shannon is quiet for several seconds. "I'll call the police as soon as we can find a phone, let them know you're safe," she says. I see Zany pat her pocket and I think of Adam's phone, but I don't say anything. "Then we can take care of the truck you *borrowed* and go straight home." I see her glance at the urn in the rearview mirror. "All of us."

So after all this, we've failed.

I wait for happiness to come. I wait to feel pleased that Zany's plan to scatter Mama Lacy in Asheville has fallen through. Like Mama Shannon and Mrs. Madison, I never wanted to let go of Mama Lacy in the first place.

But then I think: *If you want to do something, just decide to.* And Mama Lacy decided to make it back to Asheville by the time she turned forty, and instead, she never made it to forty. And Zany decided to help her, and all I've done is hold her back.

I look to Zany for guidance and to see how she's doing with the idea of not finishing what we started. She has been so strong and brave through all of this, and so certain that what she was doing was right. Her eyes are red and she's twirling her hair between her fingers. She won't meet my gaze.

Mrs. Madison keeps looking in the mirror and over her shoulder at Zany. Finally, she says, "You're wrong."

"About what?" Zany asks.

"When you said I only cared about the poodle. You were wrong. I don't always know how to say what I mean," Mrs. Madison admits, which I think is the closest she's ever come to actually saying what she means.

"I get it," I pipe up, because, suddenly, I do. "I didn't know how to say that I didn't want to live only with you. That I missed the rest of my family. Mama Shannon and Zany. I didn't know how to tell you that."

She dusts the dashboard with the back of her hand, straightens the edges of the quilt she's sitting on, un-buckles and buckles her seat belt.

"Is that why you hide out in your room and won't talk to me? Because you don't know what to say? Or because I'm not the one you want to say it to?"

"I'm not trying to hide from you!" I whisper. "I'm just—I'm sad!" Saying the word *sad* is like uncorking a bottle and tears start rushing out. Now Zany and I are both crying, beyond worn out. Zany tries to wipe up her own tears when she notices mine, but she can't get them stopped, and I know how she feels.

Mrs. Madison twists around in her seat and studies me for what seems like a very long time. Then she says, in a voice with no more anger in it, "I know you are, love." Her words are so matter-of-fact, so calm that I'm strongly reminded of Mama Lacy, the way she hardly ever got ruffled. She was the calm in the stormy seas of the Madison-Culvert family. For the first time, I see Mama Lacy in Mrs. Madison.

Then Mrs. Madison shifts back to being a regular old grandma. She digs around in her purse, and a moment later she produces two ancient Tootsie Rolls. She hands one each to me and Zany, patting both our hands with a smile. "There we go."

Mama Shannon makes eye contact with me in the rearview mirror, then looks back at the road. A minute later she does it again and I remember to thank Mrs. Madison for the candy.

Zany does, too, but quieter. She and Mrs. Madison keep sneaking glances at each other.

"Zoey Grace," Mrs. Madison says after a while, "I do care a lot about something besides the poodle. And not just Fella, either." Miles keep slipping by outside while she stares at us. "I greatly admire the people Lacy loved.

I just don't feel entitled to—to show how much I care for Zoey Grace and . . . and others. Since we're not all kin."

"But we are kin," I say. "She's my kin and you're my kin, so you two are kin. Mama Shannon, too. And family takes care of family. That's what Mama Lacy said in her letter. She said to take care of her family. She told me that."

We roll on a little while.

"I'd like to see her letter again," Mrs. Madison says softly. I remember with guilt that there is a section for Mrs. Madison, too.

"So would I," Mama Shannon says. This is the first time she's spoken for miles. Her hands are tight on the wheel, while Mrs. Madison's pet and pet at Haberdashery, who wiggles to get away. Even though she tries to hold him, he squirms free and crawls into my lap. His company gives me the courage to speak.

"I . . . have it."

Zany twists away to get a better look at me.

"Sorry," I say. "I . . . needed something."

Mama Shannon lets out a long, shaky breath. "We all needed something." She doesn't sound mad anymore, just sad. There are too many mixed-up feelings in the car. Anger and confusion and heartache. I feel like we're at sea and any second a wave is going to wash us all away.

Mrs. Madison purses her lips and looks among the three of us. Then she cradles Haberdashery tighter as she turns to stare out the windshield. Once or twice I see her shoulders jump. I'm terrified that my grandmother is crying by herself up front.

"I wish you'd told me, Ophelia," Mrs. Madison says to the dashboard, "how strongly you felt about all this. I know you were hesitant to come live with me in the beginning, but I just wanted to keep you safe and cared for. Nobody tells me anything. They expect me simply to know."

I know how Mrs. Madison feels. People are all the time expecting me to understand things I can't get my brain around. Like how to be brave, or how to find the right words to say what's on my mind. Like how to accept that somebody could die and be gone when I wasn't finished loving them yet.

We've reached the exit. I lean past Zany to get a better look. She's pressed to the window, which is down, letting the February air in, because Zany is trying to capture enough water to wash the tears off her face. I'm amazed Mrs. Madison hasn't insisted that she roll up the window yet.

We're almost on top of the sign before I make out what it says:

I look for the little white number to tell me how far we fell short of our goal. Or how close we came. Instead, as we flash past the sign, all I see is a crooked arrow pointing toward our exit, and my heart starts to pound.

This is Asheville.

We've arrived hours later than we expected, in a different car than we left in, and with more people than we'd planned on. We've arrived cold, wet, tired, muddy, and drained. We've arrived—or at least I have—uncertain of what is the best thing to do for Mama Lacy.

I know Mama Shannon only intends to turn around. But this is Asheville! This is home!

Turning around or not—angry mother at the wheel or not—I feel a rush of relief that we've arrived. I feel like maybe we can do other hard things, too, if only we do them together.

chapter
24

I think the city skyline will be un-familiar after all these years, but right away I recognize the softness of it, how it doesn't tower like some cities, all serious and important. It only raises its arms above its head a bit, like a little kid playing in the rain. The buildings are just tall enough so that you know you've arrived.

One highway gives way to another, so it takes Mama Shannon a few tries to find a suitable place to turn around. She drives up a ramp onto a smaller road and pulls into the first parking lot she finds.

Zany's still sniffling, and I nudge her. "Zany!" Trying to get her to sit up and look. But she won't even glance at me and her fingers have uncurled from the urn. I take it from her.

Mama Shannon sighs as she swings us in a slow circle and puts on her turn signal, back the other way. I crane my neck to gaze at the city skyline, and all at once I have this memory of being lifted. Of Mama Lacy showing me out the window of our apartment above the warehouse, "That's our city, Fella Sweets. That's where I want to live always." I remember thinking that if Mama Lacy wanted to live there always, so did I. With buildings so pretty and my family beside me, there would never be any reason to leave.

And now we're about to leave Asheville without ever setting foot outside the car, without doing what we came here to do. Mama Lacy will go back on the mantel and I'll go back to bed in my big, empty room at Mrs. Madison's. Mama Lacy's birthday will pass and her dying wish, which is the closest thing she'll ever have to another birthday wish, won't come true. And if anybody bothers to bake a cake, which nobody will, we will have to put thirty-nine candles on it because Mama Lacy will always be thirty-nine, even someday when I'm thirty-nine, and she'll never need another candle, ever.

Zany is hiccupping and Mama Shannon's hands on the wheel are shaking and Mrs. Madison, Mrs. Madison is going to keep me, not because she's mean and evil like Zany thinks and not because she's lonely and desperate like I've been telling myself. But because I never told her she shouldn't. I never made it clear what I wanted.

I know, right this second, what I want. But first I've got to take care of what Mama Lacy wanted. *If you want to do something, just decide to.*

I want to do something.

I push on Zany, but she won't budge. So I do the only thing I can think of. I roll my window down like Zany. Then, as Mama Shannon waits for a chance to pull out onto the road, I lift Haberdashery to the window and I set him gently out on the hillside.

"Oh no!" I shout. "Haberdashery jumped out the window!" And I kick my door open to go after him, carrying Mama Lacy along with me.

chapter
25

It's been a long time since I've been
alone. I mean alone alone, not the kind of alone I usually feel at Mrs. Madison's. Actually, come to think of it,
I'm not sure I've ever been this alone. Out in the bright
morning, in a city I haven't seen in five years, alone except for a dognapped poodle and a shiny brass urn.

The front of my mind—the part that nags at Zany to
drive slower and drink less Mountain Dew—is screaming, "I'm not so sure this is a good idea," and "You're
crazy, Fella, turn around before it's too late," and "Something bad might happen if you do this. Go back. Go
back!"

I don't go back.

The quickest way to get out of sight of my family is

to get off the road, so I cut through parking lots. I duck behind cars. I slip down alleys, feeling every bit like a criminal, cradling the urn in the crook of my arm. If the cops see me now, they would definitely arrest me, because clearly I'm doing something wrong. I think everybody in a five-mile radius must be able to hear my heart.

Because in the back of my mind, this feeling is welling up that I like. It makes my feet fly so fast, they barely touch the ground as I run. I think if the feeling rushing through me were a sound, it would be Mama Lacy singing: *The sound of people saying, I love you . . .*

I can't see the skyline anymore, now that I've run down between the buildings. I'd forgotten how steep the hills are, how all the streets and alleys and the sides of buildings lean down into valleys and swoop back up onto mountains. How much your legs can ache and your lungs can burn when you travel this city on foot. Haberdashery's getting so heavy in my grip that I have to set him on his paws and let him trot alongside me. He bravely jogs on his three good legs and I make a mental note to give him a whole jar of peanut butter later.

I'm so dizzy with freedom, and so worn out with running, that it takes me all the way to the top of the hill to realize I have no idea where I'm going. I was seven last time I was here, and I didn't pay attention to street signs. I don't see any warehouses, or anything that looks especially familiar.

Half running through the city, panting for breath but afraid to slow down, I'm able to name the major landmarks, of course: the courthouse, and then a few blocks on, the Vance Monument stretching up toward the sky. Down one hill and up another, I find myself on a brick street I recognize, with its giant iron sculpture and its little bookstore, though some of the stores are different and others are empty. A block over, I pass a park, and I remember playing there with somebody's spotted puppy. The streets are getting more familiar now. I know I walked this way when I was small. But I can't remember how I got here, or which direction I was coming from.

I jog another block, then two. The buildings start getting smaller again and there is less pavement and more grass, first a few blades, then a little patch or two, and then the houses have actual lawns and I know I'm heading down into the residential area.

But we didn't live in that area, did we? We lived where there were stores and businesses, because we lived above a warehouse. This can't be right.

"Mama Lacy," I say in a voice hardly big enough to reach all the way out of me, let alone make it up to wherever she may be. "I need you to show me where to go, okay?"

I'm thinking this is stupid and probably even the poodle would do a better job than me at getting un-lost, and then I turn a corner and I'm looking at a purple door. A purple door that I know will lead to a room with an orange floor.

I try the door, but it's locked like most stores at this hour on a Sunday morning. I ought to keep moving. Keep running so I won't get caught.

Except I know this purple door. I remember bursting through this door a hundred times, but I don't remember where I was coming from and I'm afraid to walk away and lose this landmark.

Now that I'm no longer running, I'm starting to feel strange, anyway. Sluggish. I have to keep blinking my eyes, scrubbing at them with my knuckles. It's partly the weariness from a long night of travel and almost no sleep, and partly the chill I'm sure I'm catching from running around half-dressed in the cold for so long.

I sit down on the sidewalk and lean back against the purple door, cradling Haberdashery on my lap. When I close my eyes, I right away start having those dreams a person gets when you're very tired, the kind where you're tripping and falling and it wakes you up. Except instead of tripping and falling, I'm dropping Mama Lacy's urn, over and over. Each time I try to catch it, but it's too late, and Mama Shannon is mad.

Even when I force my eyes open and face the world awake, I know Mama Shannon is mad. Her words are circling in my head: "Do you not understand how you can't do that to a person?"

"I ran out here," I tell Haberdashery, "because I didn't want to go home and put Mama Lacy back on the mantel. I can't do that to her. But what about Mama Shannon? I was going to scatter the ashes, and I can't do that to her. What does that leave? Who should I listen to?"

Haberdashery wags his nub tail when I put him down. He walks circles around my feet at the end of his duct-tape leash. He doesn't answer. I gaze at the sky, which is bright blue, dripping with sunlight. There are clouds, the sketchy kind that my fifth-grade teacher calls stratus but Mama Lacy called painter's clouds because they look like they were painted on with the very tip of an artist's brush.

I think about how I asked Mama Lacy to show me where to go, and maybe she heard me because this familiar purple door popped up right away.

And if she heard me then, maybe she can hear me all the time, like Zany says.

I don't know if I believe it, but just in case, I whisper, "Mama Lacy, please help me figure out what I'm supposed to do with you." And I hug the brass urn tight.

For a minute I think Mama Lacy's about to answer me because somebody clears their throat, but it's a man's throat clearing and so I think maybe it's God or the police and maybe I'm in trouble. I'm too tired to be properly startled, but when I look up, there's this guy wearing a trench coat and a stripey hat like the Cat in the Hat would wear, and his eyes are nothing but smiles.

"'Sakes," he says. "Not warm enough for that getup, girl. Best get in here where there's hot cocoa." Then he puts the key in the purple door and opens up Mack and Morello's.

chapter
26

Mack and Morello's isn't called Mack
and Morello's anymore. It's called the Happy Thought
Coffee Shop, and there's a picture above the door of
Peter Pan flying through the air, holding a cup of coffee.
The inside smells like coffee beans and chocolate muf-
fins, and you can barely see the orange-painted concrete
under patches of different-colored tile. But the same old
bell rings to announce our entrance.

"Your dog has to stay near the door," the guy in the
hat says. "Dogs aren't really allowed, but I let them in as
far as the bookcase. Dogs are people, too."

"Not this one. This one's a devil." I can't imagine
which bookcase he means, since there are at least ten of
them around the coffee shop, but I drop Haberdashery's

leash near the entrance and he settles down in a circle and goes to sleep right away, looking, to be honest, not at all like a devil. Poor dog, I think he's as tired as I am. He looks like he could use a happy thought. I can't stop myself from bending down and scratching between his ears.

Past the rug Haberdashery chose as a bed, I don't see a whole lot that's familiar. The tables, the chairs, the giant, fluffy old sofas with throw pillows so dusty Mrs. Madison would have them sent out with the trash—I don't think any of this furniture was here the last time I was.

Still, something stirs deep in my memory. Something about the shape of the room. I think I taste Heath bar ice cream for a second. I remember that the menu had a cartoon picture of a wiener dog.

"My name's Luther," the guy in the Dr. Seuss hat says. I'm not sure whether I expected him to be Mack or Morello, but I'm pretty sure we never knew anybody named Luther. I guess it makes sense, since the store's changed names. It must have changed owners, too. "Do you want a brownie for breakfast, or cake?"

He's trying to be nice, but the mention of cake makes me sad. The cake he's offering is straight from the freezer and still has ice crystals on the frosting. I'm thinking of thirty-nine candles, but even one would crack this frosting in a thousand places and it would never fit together right again.

"Just coffee," I say, sounding tougher than I feel. "And maybe something for my dog?"

"Coffee. Whatever you say, Little Sister." Luther puts on a pot of coffee so huge even Zany couldn't drink it by herself. "Two minutes," he says, and continues pulling things out of the freezer to put in the pastry case.

I occupy my two minutes wandering the store, poking at the wallpaper, scuffing at the floor. There's a feeling in me that's part wishing, part relief, and part something I don't have a name for.

"Coffee's up," Luther says, and hands me a mug that is more milk than coffee. He warms up a spinach-and-goat-cheese breakfast wrap for himself and one for Haberdashery, then puts on a second pot of coffee, this one marked DECAF.

"Sure you don't want to eat?" he asks.

"Nah. I mean, yeah. I'm sure." I sit cross-legged on the floor beside the dog and pet him, enjoying his company because he's the only truly familiar thing in a place that is full of half memories.

Luther startles me, asking, "You're one of the girls that's been on TV, right? I recognize the poodle." And before I can deny it, "Where's your sister?"

"I don't know what—oh—fine. Zany's with our mama. They found us—or we found them—but then I—I had one more thing I had to do."

Luther starts taking the chairs down from the tables. He's awfully calm for someone who's just recognized his customer as a missing child off the news. None of the chairs match, but it makes things look cozy. I wish Zany were here. I'm sure she needs another cup of coffee by now, and she could explain things to Luther better than I can. I wonder how long he's going to give me before he calls the police to report me found. But I don't ask him, because I'm distracted by the muted TV and its picture of me and Zany.

In the picture, we're only a little bit younger and I'm smiling at the camera and Zany's smiling at me. And then I get it, like that stupid cartoon lightbulb springing on above my head. Zany's the one who brought us here, ashes and all. Zany's the one I can't do this without.

And Mama Shannon, too. And Mrs. Madison.

"Hey, Luther?" I ask. "Can I use your phone? I got to fix something."

He clicks on the cordless phone and hands it across the counter. I listen to the dial tone for a minute. It takes three tries to dial Information correctly, and two more to get my voice to spit out my question properly. But pretty soon the phone is ringing at the hospital in Wytheville.

They patch me through to Adam's dad's room and Adam sounds terrified when he picks up. In fact, I'm surprised he picks up at all. "Mom?" he says. "Before you start screaming, listen a second. I had to—"

"It's not Mom," I interrupt, "it's Fella."

"Oh!" He swears. Then, "You scared me!"

"Sorry. I wasn't trying to scare you. I need your phone number." I rock my head to crack my neck, shaking the tired loose. Luther's watching from behind the counter so he can take the phone when I'm done.

"You what?" Adam asks.

"Your phone number. I need it."

There's a pause. Then, "You and Zany didn't get separated, did you?"

"If you call me running away from her separated, then yeah. But I need to find her."

"Fella, you're all alone?"

"I'm fine. I'm in a coffee shop and this guy Luther's real nice. How's your dad?" I can't believe it wasn't the first thing I asked.

"He's hanging on," Adam says in the kind of voice where I know he doesn't even realize he's answering the question. He gives me his number and says, "Call back if she doesn't answer and we'll figure something out."

"Thanks, Adam."

"Yeah." He hangs up first, and quickly, and I know he must want to get his attention back to his father. I smile at Luther as I click the phone off and back on to dial Zany.

She answers on half a ring. "Hello?"

"It's me."

"It's her!" Zany relays. There's a rustle and then Mama Shannon's voice comes on the line, shrill and shaky. "Ophelia Madison-Culvert!"

I take a page out of Adam's book and blurt, "Before you start screaming, listen a sec—"

But it's too late. She's already screaming. "Where are you? Were you trying to give us all a heart attack, Fella? We'll come get you. Are you safe? Tell me where you are! *How* many times in a single *day* can you give your mother a heart attack?"

When she pauses for breath, I seize the opportunity. "Before I tell you where I am, you have to promise—"

"I will do no such thing!" Mama Shannon doesn't even wait to find out what I want her to promise. She's beyond hysterical. I hear Mrs. Madison's voice in the background, and Zany's, too, but I can't tell what they're saying over Mama Shannon's yelling. "You're trying to make demands now? You'll tell me where you are *if*? Young lady, that is simply not how it works! I did not raise you to—to steal a dead woman's ashes and make ransom demands! Do you hear the sentences coming out of my mouth? Do you *hear* how far outside the lines you are? And you'll tell me where you are *if*?"

There's no room for an answer, so I simply wait. The next time she draws a breath, which is so long I figure she must be three shades of blue by now, I say, "Mama, I need you to promise." My voice is quieter than hers and this seems to give her a moment's pause. She quiets, too, a little.

"Fella, *what*?"

"Promise we'll scatter Mama Lacy, okay? All together. Zany's right. It's what she wanted. What she asked for in her letter." I have gained a new respect for people who are brave enough to ask for what they want.

There's a long sigh on the other end of the phone, and something that sounds so much like a sob that my own eyes tear up at the sound of it.

"Why?" she asks. Mama Shannon has always been so strong and so happy. Although it's been six months, I'm still not used to hearing her voice sound small.

"Because she didn't get to hike the Appalachian Trail," I say. "And she didn't get to sing in front of people."

"Oh, Fella."

"We kept her, and it's okay. I know she wanted us to keep her. But we kept her and she stayed with us and she didn't do all those things she wanted to do in her lifetime."

"She wanted *us*," Mama Shannon says. "She wanted to be with us, kiddo. I swear she did."

"I know. I know she did, only people can want more than one thing. I want to keep her ashes where I can feel like she's with me. But I also want to do what she asked us to do. And I think that matters more."

I hear her sigh or sob, I'm not sure which, and then she goes on. "Okay, you're right. I know you're right. We will do what she wanted."

"Promise."

"I promise."

"Mrs. Madison has to promise, too."

"She promises."

"Mama—"

"Okay, okay." There's another rustle and a pause. Then my grandmother's voice comes on the phone.

"Fella—"

She starts to say more, but I beat her to it. One slow

sentence at a time, I tell her exactly what I've been meaning to say—what I've been frightened to say—all this time.

"Three things," I tell her.

"What's the first?" Mrs. Madison helps me organize my own thoughts.

"We have to scatter Mama Lacy. We have to. I know you want to keep her. I want to keep her, too. But she doesn't belong on a mantel in the dark. She belongs outside in the air. That's what she would want. That's what she *did* want, and she told us. Okay?"

There's a pause. Then, "Two?"

"Twenty dollars is a lot of money."

"Well . . . okay. What makes you say that?"

"I just wanted to remind you." I don't add, *and myself.*

"And the third thing?" she asks after a minute.

"We're a family," I say. "All of us. Okay?"

There's a small sigh. "Well, I never said we weren't."

"So after we give Mama Lacy her birthday wish, we all go home together."

"Well, of course. We only have one car."

Now she reminds me of Zany and I huff an impatient sigh. "I don't mean the car. I mean we all go *home* together. Your house is the size of a library, and we're a family. We're supposed to be together. Okay?" There's quiet and I'm afraid I've asked too much. My heart pounds and my mouth gets dry, but I make the words come out anyway. "You told me you can't just know things, that people have to tell you what they want. Well, I want Mama Shannon. And I want Zany. And I want you, too."

"Oh." Such a little sound, with so much inside it. Then she says, in a brisk voice more like herself, "If we can talk your mother into it, I believe that is a wonderful solution."

I'm quick to uphold my end of the bargain. "Tell Mama Shannon I'm at Mack and Morello's," I say, heart pounding so hard my hands won't hold still. "It was the closest thing I could find to home."

chapter
27

Mama Lacy loved walking. I remember being so little I had to reach up above my head to hold her hand. I know in my head she was small for a grown-up—Mama Shannon was always teasing her for being a tiny little person, "put together out of wire and fairy dust," she would say. It's funny how I can remember those words, but when I picture Mama Lacy, I picture her big. Sometimes she's so big, she takes up the whole image.

"Spirited," that's what Mama Lacy called Mama Shannon. She used to gaze at her, a half smile on her lips. "That's my spirited lady." Usually when Mama Shannon was getting mad or hyped up about something. But it's Mama Lacy who I think was spirited, Mama Lacy, whose energy and strength and beauty are still splashed into every shadow on this sidewalk that shouldn't be familiar after all these years. I remember walking here with Mama Lacy. I remember her singing about sunshiny days while her warm hand kept mine from the cold.

It's February, and tomorrow will be March, and spring will come without my Mama Lacy to share it with. She will never take me for a springtime walk just to watch the cherry blossom petals blow across the sidewalk like warm snow. She will never explain which bird is which by their song. She will never again drink iced coffee before it's quite warm enough, sling her sweater across my shoulders so the breeze can breathe across her skin. The whole world will turn green and sweet and warm, and my mama will stay still and gone.

She won't be trapped, though. If she can't walk in spring, at least she can be free of the heavy urn that has grown so familiar in my hands.

Zany and I take turns leading the way. I take big steps, remembering being little and trying to keep up. When I forget where to go, Zany edges ahead. We take turns, too, with the things in our hands. I take the phone from her and give her the urn. A while later, she lets me take it back. We keep Mama Lacy between us. Mama Shannon and our grandmother follow behind.

We stop at the base of the hill, where there's a fancy new bakery with curlicue wrought-iron fencing and a patio with umbrella tables. It's not open yet and everything smells like sawdust and paint. Beyond it, what's left of the lawn stretches down to the main road, where cars slide by without ever caring that they're passing something very different from what used to be here.

"Where is it?" Zany asks.

Nobody answers, because it's clear where our home above the warehouse is. It isn't anywhere. It doesn't exist anymore. The whole building is gone, torn down and replaced. We're left standing here looking at how Mama Lacy's last wish might not come true after all.

I'm ready to start crying, and I think Zany might, too, and then Mama Shannon beats us to it, silent and pitiful, eyes closed and shoulders shaking. She tries not to let on, but there's no mistaking the tiny gasps and hiccups, and Zany and I are startled right out of our tears. I wrap my arms around Mama Shannon's right arm and Zany takes her left and we hold her up like that, waiting for her to tell us what to do, but she never does.

I think I know anyway.

I slip my hands from Mama Shannon's and I walk around to Zany, who is cradling the brass urn, loose. I take it from her, and kiss it, and walk back up the hill toward the Happy Thought.

The walk up the hill is much slower than the walk down. Not just because of the hill, but because I remember so much of this walk, I keep wanting to look at things. Plenty has changed about our city in five years, but plenty has stayed the same, too. Walking here, where Mama Lacy walked so many times with us, I feel like she is with me, not in the brass jar in my hands, but in the city coming alive around us. It's cold, but the sun is up and people are starting to come out of their homes. People are walking dogs. Biking. A man is playing guitar on the sidewalk. I hear Mama Shannon working on getting her breath back to normal so she doesn't sound like she's been crying, and I hear Haberdashery sniffing along the sidewalk for the exact right blade of grass to pee on. It's normal and comforting.

They let me lead the way, all the way up the hill until I stop.

"Here?" Mama Shannon asks.

"It's the closest thing I could find to home," I repeat.

When we scatter Mama Lacy's ashes on the lawn of the Happy Thought Coffee Shop, she doesn't catch the wind and blow away like I had pictured. Instead she works her way down into the blades of soft grass on the hillside. It looks to me like she's settling in, now that we've brought her home.

At times like these, I think you're supposed to say a few words. I can hear Mama Shannon whispering, and Zany's talking under her breath.

But me, I don't have to say anything. There's nothing I can say that Mama Lacy doesn't know already.

chapter
28

After a while, I notice that my robe pocket is ringing. My family doesn't look ready to move just yet, so I take a step away before I answer.

"Adam?"

He's quiet too long, and I know.

"When?" I ask. My voice breaks.

"A few minutes ago."

"Were you with him?"

"Yeah."

"Did you say the right thing?" I know this was important to him.

Adam laughs a short, sad laugh. "What you told me was right, Fella, it didn't matter what I said. So yeah, I said the right thing."

"Okay." I look out across the hillside, take in Mama Lacy's final home. Take in the family she's left behind, stronger now because of her.

"Okay," I repeat. "Wait for us, we're coming back. I got a few more things to tell you."

Author's Note

"**We could have pushed for both our** names on the paperwork." Jane's fixing the doorknob with distracted motions. Her hands seem to know what she's doing without her mind, which is miles away and years in the past, answering my question. As the head of one of the few families in the area to have pursued adoption as a same-sex couple, she is happy to answer my questions, but unfortunately, not all of them have easy answers.

"They advised us not to list both our names. Said it was less complicated, more likely to go through if it was only one of us. If it was only me. I can't get this thing to . . ." She trails off, lets the screwdriver rest mid-air, looks out across the river to the train tracks against the far mountain. We're standing in my rental house, which is the house where Jane's family lived when she first brought home her children. The house is rented out now that she and the children's other mom have parted ways—the closest word is *divorce*, although neither the divorce nor the marriage before it carries any legal weight. "We could have pushed for both of us to be on the paperwork, but it wasn't about us. It was about three kids who needed parents."

To those unfamiliar with the time line of same-sex marriage and parenting, Jane's description sounds like something that happened in the distant past. The truth is, it's not even been a decade. Jane's kids are playing outside. Now ranging in age from nine to thirteen, they don't remember much about those early days when their moms were fighting to adopt them. What they know now is that they have two loving, devoted mothers—only one of whom is their parent, as far as the law is concerned.

Families like Jane's have long faced challenges when it comes to protecting themselves and their children. In the United States, gay marriage has only been legal in all fifty states since June 26, 2015. Before that date, the rights a couple or a family had and the challenges they faced depended on the state they lived in. The Madison-Culvert family lived in two states, North Carolina and West Virginia, where gay marriage wasn't legal until 2014.

Sometimes it seems like the changes have happened

very quickly. After all, when I wrote *Ashes to Asheville* in 2010, I never dreamed I would have to go back and rewrite it to take place in the recent past. I assumed that when the book was ready to hit the shelves, same-sex marriage would still be a piecemeal affair, and the rights of couples like Lacey and Shannon to marry, make health-care decisions, parent as a unit, and do all the things the opposite-sex couple across the street could do would depend largely on what state they lived in. It was a happy surprise to find myself rewriting parts of the novel to change the time line because the rights of same-sex couples had outpaced my expectations.

Still, for some, the changes came very slowly. For a lot of couples in the United States over the past several decades, the reality was that, even after jumping through every legal hoop they could find, they were still frequently left unable to add each other to their health insurance plan, file taxes as a couple, make medical decisions for each other in the face of catastrophic health events, or adopt each other's children.

"Got it," Jane says, wiggling the doorknob to make sure it's really locked. "That ought to hold." I think about how many times she's had to say something similar, carefully arranging paperwork in favor of adopting her children, making promises to her fellow parent with no legal weight, and wiggling them to make sure they'll hold. I think of how her family lacks the protection of a family just now starting a similar journey. I think about how it's families like Jane's, quietly living their lives, that have pushed for a more fair circumstance for other families across the nation.

"Thanks," I say, not just for fixing the door, but for being one of the families who helped open doors for everyone.

Acknowledgments

I'm extremely grateful to a lot of people for their help with the crazy road trip that has been *Ashes to Asheville*. Stacey Barney, Kate Meltzer, and the folks at Putnam are skilled mechanics wielding an arsenal of tools and talent, and the book starts up and runs thanks to their work. Laura Langlie paints the road signs and makes sure I can find them, pointing out the turns when I'm driving in the dark.

At the stops for gas or pie or coffee, I've met fellow travelers. There are Stacie, Matt, and the kids; Carrie and her girls; Jane and the VanCross kids, particularly the book's very first kid reader, Ashley; a smattering of Huntington writers; and of course Jill and Caroline, Teri, Michael, Alexis, Bev, Mike, John, Jessica, Shanna, and all the others who are driving different cars in a similar direction. As long as we're on the road together, we're all less likely to be lost.

And in my car, there are two patient parents, Mark and Kate, who manage not to turn the car around despite the shenanigans in the back. A niece and a nephew with map-reading and time-budgeting skills that surpass the lot of us, in charge of the itinerary. And two sisters, Heather and Jennifer, who have grown up to be confident, witty, and wise sources of strength and inspiration . . . no matter what shape I thought their heads were when I was six. (For the record, their heads were flat rocks. Also, it's their fault I can't spell *encyclopedia*.) I love you both to absolute bits.

John McCoy

Sarah Dooley is the critically acclaimed author of *Free Verse*. She has lived in an assortment of small West Virginia towns, each of which she grew to love. Winner of the 2012 PEN/Phyllis Naylor Working Writer Fellowship, she has written two additional novels for middle-grade readers, *Body of Water* and *Livvie Owen Lived Here*. Sarah is a former special education teacher who now provides treatment to children with autism. She lives in Huntington, West Virginia, where she inadvertently collects cats. She's a 2006 graduate of Marshall University.